SUMMER'S STOLEN

A SEASONS OF MAGIC URBAN FANTASY NOVEL

SARAH BIGLOW

For information contact; www.sarah-biglow.com

Editing and Formatting by: Under Wraps Publishing Services

Cover Design by: Deranged Doctor Design

ISBN: 978-1-955988-92-6

Published by Sarah Biglow: 2020

10 9 8 7 6 5 4 3 2 1

 Formatted with Vellum

SPECIAL THANKS

This edition was made possible by the support of so many wonderful backers on Kickstarter.

But I wanted to say a special thank you to **Myrdd, Clair John, Bill Lisse, Joe G., Jay A. Reynolds, Beth Wrege, Gerald P. McDaniel, Kandi, Lav, Kaitlyn, Cynthia Coffman, Kevin S. Varner, Jeffrey Tristan Thyme, Deborah Hedges, Stacy Shuda, Ryan Scott James, Mothy, Meredith, Seamus Sands and Tommy** for helping the campaign and these books soar higher than I ever imagined possible.

JUNE 19, 2017

ONE

I stared up at the Authority's imposing building that until a few short months ago had only been a bad memory from my childhood. Still a lot had changed for the better since I'd learned the truth about my mother's death—she'd given her life to protect me until I could fulfill my destiny—realizing that the Authority wasn't the heartless conspirators I'd long believed them to be. In some ways, her death had shaped me into the Savior everyone needed to stop the Order of Samael from raising druids from the dead.

"Unless you've learned how to astral project, I'm pretty sure you have to go inside for the council meeting," a familiar baritone voice said from behind me.

I turned to look at Desmond, my cousin, and grinned. "Not yet. I'll add it to my to do list, right after teleportation," I quipped. We could do a lot of amazing things with magic, but even it had limits.

The noontime sun beat down on us and he wiped sweat from his forehead. Spring had been mild and it was shaping up to be a cooler summer than we'd had in years. I'd hoped stopping the Order from raining terror down on all of us three months ago would have restored the balance of nature, but signs of the imbalance lingered. At least we were only three days from the Summer Solstice. Light magic would be at its height and I was eager to feel the surge in my own power. A voice crackled over the radio on my belt, calling out codes for crimes currently in progress. I was off duty and lowered the volume.

"I guess we better go inside," I said gesturing to the front doors.

I followed Desmond inside and up the staircase to the second-floor meeting room. I nudged the door open all the way to reveal thirteen chairs laid out in a semi-circle, about half of them filled. Thirteen members had occupied the council since the time of the Witch Trials when the Authority was founded. Until I'd come back into the fold, they'd operated with only twelve members.

I barely had time to sit down when Belladonna Montes—one of the Authority's healers—descended upon me. She was a kind woman and had helped me recover from some serious scrapes. Worry lines pinched her mouth and the corners of her eyes. She took the seat meant for Desmond and he moved off, sensing Belladonna wanted some privacy.

"Is everything okay?" I asked.

She shook her head. "It's Adrian. I haven't heard from in a couple days."

Her teenage son had been training to take up the mantle of healer like his mother. I'd only had a few interactions with him, but he seemed like a good kid. "Are you sure he isn't just crashing with friends?"

"No. He was supposed to be with a friend three days ago, but I called. His friend's parents said he never showed up. I wasn't expecting him home until last night. When he didn't come home, I got worried."

I knew she was telling me, because I was a cop. For a long time, I'd been police first and a witch second. These days I was trying to find a better balance of my inherited family traits with the career I'd chosen. "We usually have to wait at least twenty-four hours for someone to be missing before anything can be done officially. Still, if you give me his cell phone number I'll see if I can find him." I patted her arm. "Relax. Kids act out and take off sometimes. Lord knows I did when I was his age." *Although he hadn't come home to find his mother dead in the living room with a knife in her chest.*

"Adrian has never been a wild kid, Ezri. Though ..." She trailed off.

"What?" I prompted.

"He's been spending a lot more time online lately. I told myself it was nothing. Although what if something happened to him, because of someone he met online?"

It wasn't out of the realm of possibility. Crime in social media was a whole new world for us and we were desperately playing catch up. I knew bailing on the meeting would be frowned upon, but I also knew that I needed to put Belladonna's mind at ease as soon as possible. "What's his cell number? I'll get on it right away," I said pulling out a notepad and pen.

"What about the meeting?" She gestured at the gathered people.

"They survived without me for years. I think they can handle one meeting on their own," I answered.

She nodded, and taking the pad and pen from me, scribbled down her son's phone number. I stood, pocketed the pad and started for the far end of the room that led into a well-concealed tech hub. I felt a hand on my arm before I reached the threshold. I grabbed the wrist joint as I spun, facing a startled Desmond on the other end of the arm. I let go.

"Sorry," I apologized.

"Where are you going?" He asked, massaging his wrist.

"To put a mother's mind at ease and to do that I need to pay a visit to your girlfriend," I answered.

"Let me know if I can help," Desmond said.

I gave him a nod and disappeared through the doorway. Thankfully Avery sat at the bank of computers. Until three months ago, I never realized the Authority had their own version of tech support. After helping to crack a serial murder case, Avery had accepted a freelance gig with Boston PD, which wasn't a secret. So, why hadn't Belladonna gone straight to Avery? *Because Avery isn't the Savior.*

"Knock, knock," I said, announcing my presence.

Avery spun in her chair to face me with a pair of headphones slung around her neck. She was petite and blonde. Not what I would have pegged as my cousin's type—before our decade-long separation he'd only dated brunettes—but she was whip smart and snarky. She'd quickly grown on me, too.

"Hey, Ez. Aren't you supposed to be in a big, important council meeting?" She asked, gesturing back towards the way I'd come.

I shrugged one shoulder. "I've got more pressing concerns." I pulled the pad from my pocket and handed it over. "I need you to give me a GPS location on this phone number."

Avery quirked a brow at me as she turned back to her computer setup. "And you didn't go to the actual police with this, because?"

"Because I wanted to keep it in-house," I answered, hoping she caught the meaning behind my words.

"You going to tell me who I'm looking for and why?"

"Right now, I'm just hoping it's a kid out for a joyride or sleeping off a bender too afraid to go home and face the consequences." God, my words made me sound so old. I was only ten years older than Adrian.

Avery said nothing else, instead focusing her attention on the screen in front of her. I picked up the now-familiar scent of her magic—cinnamon—as she gave the search an added boost. Some people were born to be healers. Me, I got the ability to pick up on a person's magical signature. Sure, even that power had boundaries. If it had been more than twenty-four hours it was basically useless. I'd been honing that particular skillset for the last three months though. Now I could stretch that period to nearly thirty hours.

"Got it," Avery said about five minutes later.

"Where?" I leaned over her shoulder, trying to study the grid-like map in front of me.

"Near Atlantic Avenue, I'd guess it's probably somewhere near South Station. I can't get any closer than that even with the magic boost."

"What if I called it?"

She shook her head. "I mean, if you were actually there then maybe that would work. Given the size of the station, from here it's useless."

At least I knew where I was heading. "Thanks.

I'm going to head there now, so stick around in case we need you."

"We?" Avery glanced at me from over her shoulder.

"Me and Jacquie." I had a partner to grab.

TWO

South Station was one of the busiest travel hubs in Boston, save for Back Bay Station and Logan International Airport. It housed not only two branches of the transit system, but train and bus services, too. I stood above ground near one of the entrances to the station when a tall, caramel-skinned woman approached me.

"So, you want to tell me what we're doing here on our day off?" Jacquie DeWitt, my partner, asked. We'd been partnered for almost five months now. When she'd first been assigned as my partner after earning my Detective's shield, I hadn't known that she knew my magical secret. There'd been some tension and hurt feelings on my part when I'd learned the truth three months ago. Now, I couldn't imagine the world without her having my back even on all things magical.

"Belladonna Montes thinks her son, Adrian, is missing. I said I'd look into it for her. We tracked his cell to this general area," I explained.

Most people were oblivious to the existence of magic in the world. We were all safer that way. I counted myself lucky every day that Jacquie wasn't most people.

"Well, where do we start? T, trains or bus?" She replied.

"Avery said she had pinged his cell near Atlantic Avenue. So that makes me think trains or bus terminal," I said before heading down the stairs to the underground connection of the subway trains to the upper level that served the trains and buses. I took the stairs two at a time, popping up in the heart of the food court.

I scanned the crowds of people milling about waiting for their trains or getting lunch. I dug my phone out of my pocket and dialed Adrian's number. It rang four times before going to voicemail. I ended the call. "The phone's still on." I passed Jacquie my pad with the number on it. "I'm going to have Avery track the phone. Call it when I tell you."

Avery's line rang only one time before she answered. "Did you find who you were looking for?"

"Not yet. We're going to try calling their phone now that we're closer. Can you try to get us a more precise location?"

"I'll do my best."

I took off at a brisk walk out onto the train tracks. My instincts told me that trains weren't the right answer. If he'd hopped a train, his phone wouldn't still have a signal near the station. I moved on to the bus terminal building at the far end. I gave Jacquie a nod to place the call.

"We're calling now," I told Avery.

I stepped through the door to the first level of the terminal and took a slow breath. With my free hand, I touched the sandalwood charm at my throat, clearing Avery's magic from my senses. Crowds weren't the best place to hunt down magical signatures, but I didn't have a choice. I could smell the remnants of fast food and the general body odor of the masses in 80 degree weather, but nothing that screamed magic.

"Okay, I've managed to pull up a schematic of the terminal. Looks like the signal is above you," Avery said.

"Got it. Thanks."

I ended the call and barreled toward the escalator for the second floor, Jacquie hot on my heels. A few people gave us irritated looks as we bolted up the escalator. I flashed my badge and they stepped aside. I came to a halt in the hallway leading to the actual bus bays.

"I'll try again," Jacquie said, setting her phone to speaker.

The line rang again and this time, I picked up the faint sound of a ringtone nearby. It could have been a figment of my imagination, but I wanted to believe that we'd found Adrian and could set his mother's mind at ease.

"This way," I said, motioning for Jacquie to follow me toward the escalators up to the top level.

The sound grew louder as we approached a trash can. My heart sank as we both stopped and stared down at the edge of a cell phone haphazardly buried under fast food wrappers. Jacquie pulled a glove from her back pocket and fished out the phone. She held it up for me to see the display, her number on it with two missed calls.

"That's not good," I breathed and glanced around our surroundings. If Adrian had decided to run away, there were plenty of places to pick as a destination and at least three different bus lines, too.

"Are you able to pick up anything unusual around here?" Jacquie asked, alluding to my signature-scenting ability.

I closed my eyes letting the sweet scent of strawberries bloom around me, fueling my magic. I poured my intent out into the world around me, seeking out any foreign bits of magic.

Nothing.

"It's looking like he ran away. Even if someone did take him, they didn't use magic to do it," I answered. Belladonna had been right to worry. Now I just had to hope I could find a kid who possibly didn't want to be found.

THREE

Some habits as a cop were hard to shake like carrying evidence bags. Jacquie slid Adrian's phone into a clear plastic baggie before heading back down the concourse.

"Where are you going?" Jacquie called after me when I reached the stairs to the first floor.

"To find security. See if we can figure out what time Adrian got here and where he might have gone," I replied.

"This isn't an official case, Ezri. We can't just walk in there without a warrant demanding they show us footage." She closed the distance between us and put a hand on my shoulder. "I understand you want to help a friend, but we need to go through the appropriate channels."

I knew she was right, but that meant confirming Belladonna's fears and I wasn't sure I was ready to face her yet. "Okay. I'll go back to headquarters and fill Belladonna in. I'll get her to come down and file a missing person's report. Then we get the warrant and try to find this kid."

We headed back through the station and out to both of our cars sitting in a small lot. I hesitated with my hand on the handle of the driver side door. Jacquie gave me a smile. "You want me to come with you to break the news?'

Heat warmed my cheeks in embarrassment. I was a detective damn it. I should be able to handle this on my own. Yet, I couldn't deny having my partner there to back me up gave me a huge sense of relief. "You don't have to," I said, trying to brush aside her offer.

She shut and locked the door to her own car before rounding to the passenger side of mine. "You may be the Savior, but even saviors need moral support. Come on, get in."

I exhaled and climbed behind the wheel. The trip back to headquarters in Newton wouldn't take long at this time of day. As I drove, I glanced at Jacquie preoccupied by her phone. "Everything okay?" I prompted as I eased to a stop at a red light.

"The kids are just getting settled back with Denise. I was checking on them," she answered without looking up from the screen.

Until a few weeks ago, Jacquie's niece and nephew had been in her custody while her sister-in-law completed rehab. Even after I'd learned the extent of Jacquie's involvement in the magical community—Denise's family had magic and it was highly likely Troy and Neveah had inherited it through her bloodline—my partner still didn't like to talk about her family. She tried to keep her emotions under wraps, but I knew her well enough to tell losing them hurt. Sure, she was still in their lives, but they'd come to depend on her while she was their guardian. On the rare occasions she did talk about them, she lit up, even if she didn't realize it.

"That's got to be a big adjustment for everyone," I said.

"I know Denise put in the work to get them back ... I respect that, but I'd gotten used to having them around."

"I can't believe she wouldn't let you see them whenever you wanted," I offered as I pressed down on the accelerator.

Jacquie just nodded silently as I pulled into the circular drive of headquarters. I pulled in behind Desmond's little VW bug and killed the engine. Blowing out a breath, I tried to gather my thoughts. Jacquie was already out of the car before I'd even unbuckled my seatbelt. I followed after her, trying to sort through why Adrian might have taken off. A secret romance was one option, especially if the object of his affection wasn't someone he thought his mother would approve of. Besides it would fit with him hiding his online activity from her. Once inside, I started toward the staircase to the second floor when the door to the library on my left opened and Belladonna burst through. She zeroed in on me and descended.

"Let's talk somewhere private," I said.

Her face turned into a neutral mask, ushering me back into the library. Jacquie stepped in behind us and closed the doors. The last time I'd been in this room, I'd been bodies deep in a case hunting a gargoyle who turned out to be a scapegoat and a kid who got mixed up in things he shouldn't have. I prayed the same fate hadn't befallen Adrian.

"The fact you are both here does not inspire me with confidence," Belladonna said, her voice soft.

"We found Adrian's phone at South Station, tossed in a trash can at the bus terminal," I shared.

"What?" Her voice cracked as the word passed her lips.

"It's possible he got on a bus somewhere. In order for us to keep looking for him, we will need you to make a formal missing person's report. Then we can file for a warrant and see what we can find on the station's surveillance cameras," I explained.

"He wouldn't run away. Someone must have taken him," Belladonna insisted. She shook her head vigorously as if it would be enough to make her words a reality.

"We aren't ruling that out, but I didn't sense any

magical signatures nearby. Now, it's entirely possible he dumped his phone a couple days ago and I wouldn't be able to pick up on any signatures at that point," I said, knowing she didn't want to hear excuses. Still, I needed to manage her expectations.

She sat unmoving and silent in the chair across from me. Unshed tears sparkled in her eyes, but she didn't let them fall. "I'll file the report. Please, you have to find him."

"We can't make any promises, but we will do everything we can," I replied.

"It would be helpful if you could give us the password for his phone and access to his computer," Jacquie interjected.

"Of course. Whatever you need."

Jacquie opened the library door and ushered Belladonna out towards the front of the building. I was halfway down the front hall following after them when I spotted a familiar man wearing an EMT uniform waiting for me at the bottom of the stairs. J.T. Somers had been my high school boyfriend. I'd let my own drama push us apart for over a decade. He'd come back into my life—saving it in fact—during my first go around with the Order. Not long after that we'd fallen back into each other's arms. It was comforting to know he still loved me even after everything I'd put him through.

"Everything okay, Ez? Des said you bailed on the

council meeting," he said, leaning over and planting a kiss on my lips.

"Adrian's gone missing," I answered. J.T. was a healer like Belladonna. He might have some insight into what Adrian had been up to lately. "You wouldn't happen to know if he'd been in contact with anyone he wouldn't want his mom to know about, do you?"

He stepped off the bottom step and followed me out into the afternoon air. The temperature had risen a few degrees since I'd gone inside and I wiped sweat from the nape of my neck.

"Why do I feel like I'm being interrogated?" He said with a small smirk.

"Habit. I get on a case and my brain switches to cop mode without thinking. Seriously though, J.T., if you know anything I could really use it."

He rubbed his chin in thought. "To be honest I hadn't seen much of Adrian lately. His mom had been handling most of his training so that wasn't totally unusual. Although, he used to hang out with some of the other kids when they were getting lessons after school and I can't say I've seen him with them recently. You could check with them."

It wasn't what I'd been hoping for, but it was better than nothing. I gave him a kiss of my own. "Thanks. That helps."

He started to wrap his arms around my waist when I pulled back and took the front steps two at a time. J.T. stood there looking disappointed. "We still on for dinner tonight?" He called.

Shit, I'd forgotten about dinner. "You bet," I replied and climbed behind the wheel.

THE PRECINCT WAS BUSTLING when Jacquie and I led Belladonna into the bullpen. I didn't have a chance to ask anyone what the fuss was about before Belladonna pointed to a couple sitting at one of the desks with an officer.

"That's Carly Ramirez's parents," Belladonna said, her voice taking on a higher, more fraught note.

The name didn't sound familiar. Then again, there was a whole generation of kids I didn't know given my decade-long estrangement from the Authority. I tried to guide Belladonna away from the couple before she could interrupt them. We had our own issues to deal with. I settled in front of the computer and pulled up the form for a missing person's report, starting to type without asking for any details.

"I trust you can handle this?" Jacquie said, pulling my focus from the screen in front of me.

I glanced over my shoulder in her direction and I caught sight of her nephew, Troy, standing by the desk sergeant. "Yeah, go ahead."

That left Belladonna and I alone. "I'm just going

to need you to confirm your personal information and the last time you saw Adrian. If you can remember what he was wearing, that would be helpful, too," I said.

Belladonna's gaze hadn't moved from Mr. and Mrs. Ramirez. "You don't know them, do you?"

"There's a lot of people in the community I'm not familiar with these days. I'm trying, but sometimes it feels like a losing battle."

Belladonna diverted her attention long enough to give me the information I needed to finish the report and file it in the system. My brain also filed away the fact that Adrian's last name was Baptiste and not Montes. Now we could start digging into where he might have gone. "Belladonna, I have to ask, is there anyone in your life you think that might be capable of taking Adrian?"

"A few months ago, he started to ask about his father's side of the family. He left when Adrian was three."

I made a note of the possibility of a parental connection. After all, family was often the culprit in kidnappings. "Does he know about the magical community?" My voice lowered to a whisper out of habit.

"Of course. He has magic, but he's from a different culture. I think that's part of what led him to leave. He did not like the way we governed ourselves. The Afro-Hispanic community is much less structured. Each family handles their own children's education."

This was news to me. I had always assumed that magically inclined practitioners were all just a part of the Authority's sphere of influence. Although, her words made sense. The Authority's origins were European, but they weren't the only culture out there. I'd seen Belladonna train Adrian away from the other kids. *Why hadn't I made that connection before?* "Do you have any contact information for your ex?"

"I'll see what I can find, but I haven't heard from him in years."

"We've got some starting points now. I think you should just head home and I'll call if we find anything. In the meantime, it's entirely possible he'll come home on his own."

She gave me a sad smile. "You don't really believe that ... thank you for trying to give me hope."

I didn't know how to respond to her words as she got up and left the precinct. I looked around, but Jacquie and her nephew were nowhere to be seen. Mr. and Mrs. Ramirez remained by the other officer's desk as he headed for the printer. Curiosity got the better of me and I hit print on my own report, giving myself a plausible reason to pry. I got to the printer first and scooped up the pages waiting in the tray. Another missing person's report for their ten-year-old Carly.

"Detective, I think you've got my report there," the other officer said and reached for the pages.

I tried to commit the address where the girl had last been spotted to memory before handing over the paper. "Sorry about that."

Just as I got back to my desk, Jacquie reappeared. "Get what you needed for the report?" She made no mention of Troy's appearance at the precinct and I knew enough not to ask.

"Yeah. That couple over there is part of the magical community. Their ten-year-old daughter just went missing near Park Street Station. I didn't get a good look at the details, but I have a bad feeling. Up for another trip?"

"Lead the way."

FOUR

The area was crowded with pedestrians milling about the Common, taking the Freedom Trail tour or out for a late lunch. The homeless population, usually a staple in the area, was nowhere to be seen. Sure, summertime meant they spread out throughout the Common and surrounding area. Still I'd been hoping they might have seen something and the promise of a little cash might loosen their lips. I made a mental note of their absence as we crossed the street by Park Street Church, stopping in the middle of the path directly in front of the inbound exit.

"You sure all you got was a location? No details about how she went missing?" Jacquie prompted.

I should have just taken the report, passed it off as a printer error when my colleague had come looking for it. Or I should have copied the information, a feat a little magic could have accomplished. "I was in a hurry," I finally answered, avoiding her gaze.

I may not have put enough thought into jumping on this case before running off, but there was something I could do. I closed my eyes and slowed my breathing.

"Are you about to do what I think you are?" Jacquie hissed.

"Try to sniff out the abductor and see if they used magic? Yep," I answered.

"It's a bit public and broad daylight," she replied.

"No one's paying us any attention. Just keep your badge out of sight and pretend you are just another tourist," I told her, turning my attention back to my breathing.

With each breath, all sound vanished and the people passing us by faded to nothing until I stood alone. I opened my eyes and took in the magical currents all around me, begging me to tap into them, to have them aid me in whatever spell I needed cast.

That's the funny thing about magic. It's everywhere and it *wants* to be used. You just have to know where to look and have the gift to use it. The currents ebbed around me, bumping up against my own magic as if it were a tangible thing. I did a three-sixty on the spot, unsure of what I was looking for at first.

"I need to see whose magic has been here recently," I muttered to myself, the words were swallowed up by the world around me as soon as they left my mouth.

Apparently speaking my need was enough for the fabric of the world around me to obey. Whether it was a bonus of being the Savior or just being this close to the Solstice didn't matter. I'd take the supernatural assist. The scent of strawberry enveloped me as my own magic poured itself out of every pore in my body. Slowly, an image resolved in front of me. A young girl with what appeared to be dark curls stood amongst a throng of people waiting to cross the street in the direction of Winter Street. She had a cell phone pressed to one ear, her lips moving in a conversation I couldn't hear. The words weren't important—not yet, anyway.

My nose twitched as a new scent tickled it, something like brackish water. I moved toward the after-image of Carly and the scent grew stronger. She smiled at something said on the other end of the line before the scent of magic flared and suddenly she vanished. The phone reappeared on the ground a moment later as the crowd surged forward crossing the street.

I let out a gasp as the world came back to me. I let the smell of my own magic reassure me that I was okay and took a hit from the sandalwood charm to clear my palette. Jacquie loitered by one of the vendors selling Boston-themed t-shirts. I caught her attention and gestured for her to follow me. We wound our way through the paths in the Common until I was certain we were out of earshot of anyone who might be listening.

"Well?" Jacquie said pointedly.

"She was definitely taken and whoever did it used magic. We need to be on this case."

FIVE

"Captain, we need to be on the Ramirez case," I said, trying not to wave my hand too vigorously in Captain Beech's face.

"Trenton, I appreciate your enthusiasm, but it's my understanding you're already working a missing person's case." She replied, arching a brow at me.

Shit. "That's why. They might be related. Both kids went missing in public places near the transit system. Please, Captain, I have a hunch and I need to see it through," I bluffed.

Captain Beech looked to Jacquie who'd remained quiet since we got back to the precinct. She'd let me do the talking. "What's your take on Trenton's hunch, DeWitt?"

"Ezri's got good instincts. After all, I think we both know it was her hard work that solved the Taggart case."

The captain held her hands up in front of her to quell any further discussion. "Fine. You want the Ramirez case, it's yours. Bring that little girl home safe."

"We'll do our best, ma'am," I said, my mind already trying to sort out my plan of attack.

"That was nice work in there. Hell, I almost believed these cases could be connected," Jacquie whispered with a smirk.

"We don't know that they aren't related. After all, both of their families are part of the magical community," I countered.

"We need to interview Mr. and Mrs. Ramirez," Jacquie said.

"And we need warrants for the South Station security footage. We can have the regular guys take a look at that footage," I said, settling in at my desk to swear out an affidavit for the warrant.

"You sure you want to involve the mundane tech guys?" Jacquie whispered.

"Right now, we don't have any evidence to suggest Adrian's vanishing act was aided by magic. I know for a fact that Carly's disappearance had a magical component involved. I need Avery and her people putting their skills to work there."

"Seems you've thought of everything," she muttered and scooped up her phone out of the cradle on her desk.

I don't have anything figured out. I just couldn't

let the people in my community suffer if I had a chance to keep them safe. The big threat may be over, but they still looked to me to keep the bad guys at bay.

"Mr. and Mrs. Ramirez went home already. They've got a uniform with them. We should head over there. Something tells me we don't want to have this particular conversation here where prying eyes and security cameras could pick up things they shouldn't," Jacquie said, pulling me out of my daze.

"Right. That makes sense," I replied.

"Why don't we swing back by South Station on the way? We can execute that warrant for the security footage," Jacquie suggested.

THE TRANSIT POLICE hadn't been happy to see us when we waltzed into their office, warrant in hand. The officer on duty had grumbled about how many hours of footage we were asking for. After impressing upon him the fact we were chasing a missing kid, he'd shut up and promised to forward the footage by the end of the day to our people.

The Ramirez family lived in a modest three-bedroom apartment in Quincy. The uniform who sat on the couch when Jacquie and I entered the living room jumped to his feet.

"We've got it for now, Officer. Thanks," I said, dismissing him as politely as possible.

He nodded and leaned in close. "Fair warning, the mom's been doing some weird shit in the kitchen since we got here. I get that folks handle stress and trauma differently, but I've never seen anyone cook like that to cope."

Jacquie and I exchanged perplexed looks before making our way to the kitchen—likely the largest room in the apartment—and found Mrs. Ramirez standing over a map, the scent of Cayenne pepper thick in the air. I didn't see any in the kitchen which meant it was of the magical variety. Since it was strong enough for a normal person to sense made me nervous.

"Mrs. Ramirez," I said, hoping to get the woman's attention without startling her too much.

"Please forgive my wife, she isn't handling the stress of our daughter's abduction well," Mr. Ramirez said from the kitchen table.

"I wouldn't imagine anyone in your situation would be coping all that well," I said.

Our eyes met and his mouth hung open for a moment as recognition dawned on him. "You're Ezri Trenton."

My name was enough to draw his wife's attention. She set a pair of crystals down on the map before crowding my personal space in a seriously uncomfortable way. She grasped my shoulders and squeezed tight. "You're going to find her, aren't you?"

"I'm going to try. But, to do that, I'm going to need to ask you some questions."

"The officer who took the report already asked us everything," Mr. Ramirez said.

"I'm pretty sure he didn't ask these questions. Now, I know you told him what happened, but if you wouldn't mind just telling us again."

"I was on the phone with Carly when all of a sudden I heard static and then she was just gone," Mrs. Ramirez said.

"Your daughter is only ten. Does she go out by herself a lot?" I pressed.

"She's a very independent girl. She was going to pick up groceries for dinner. She liked to run errands for us. Claimed it made her feel grown up," Mr. Ramirez added.

"I'm assuming she took the T?"

"Yes, but she is a smart girl. She knows to pay attention to the people around her," Mrs. Ramirez insisted.

"I don't doubt that," I said. I gestured to the map and crystals on the counter. "Can I ask what you were doing? I've never seen magic like that before."

"My family line can sometimes divine information from scrying crystals. I was hoping it would work to track down Carly," Mrs. Ramirez explained.

I stepped over to the counter and studied the glittering quartz crystals in deep purple and red hues sitting in the center of a map of downtown. "Any luck?"

"No. The crystals resonate, but they won't reveal a location. It's like they can sense she's out there, but not where."

"Did Carly pick up groceries in the area often?" Jacquie probed.

"Only a few times a month," Mr. Ramirez answered.

"Oh, God ... you think someone was watching her?" Mrs. Ramirez wailed.

The thought had crossed my mind. "We're certainly looking into it. Did you or Carly know a healer named Adrian Baptiste?"

"Yes. He babysat Carly when she was little. She had a bit of a crush on him. He wouldn't do anything to hurt her," Mr. Ramirez said, his shoulders stiffening and his jaw muscles tensed.

"We don't think he did. However, he's gone missing, too. We're trying to determine if the two cases could be related. This next question is going to sound a little strange, but what does Carly's magic smell like?"

Both Mr. and Mrs. Ramirez stared at me, mouths agape. I wasn't surprised at their shock. It wasn't a typical question one got asked, even in the company we kept. "I can sense other practitioners by their magical scent. I picked up on one at the scene, but I need to know what Carly's magic smells like to make sure I'm following the right scent," I explained.

"It's daisies," Mrs. Ramirez said, her voice soft.

"Thank you." I made a note. Carly hadn't used any magic to stop her abductor which meant either she knew her kidnapper or they'd acted quickly enough to overpower her. "Did she know how to defend herself with her magic?"

"No. She was just starting to really learn how to use her gifts."

I jotted a few more notes down, intending to ask about a list of friends and family in Carly's life who might be potential suspects. Instead my phone buzzed with an incoming text from Avery. 'Get to HQ now. You need to see this.'

"We really appreciate your time. We're going to do everything we can to find Carly. We'll be in touch. In the meantime, can you put together a list of anyone in Carly's life ... friends, family, teachers. Anyone you can think of who might know who she would trust?"

"Yes. Of course. Thank you, Ms. Trenton," Mr. Ramirez said.

It's Detective. "It's all part of my job."

Jacquie stayed silent until we reached the car. "You did good in there," she commented, sliding behind the wheel.

"Carly didn't defend herself against whoever

took her. I only got one magical scent at the scene and it sure as hell wasn't daisies."

"Where to now?"

"Headquarters. Avery's got something for us."

SIX

Striding through the council meeting room with its empty semi-circle of chairs reminded me of the first time I'd met Avery. Desmond had dragged me back here, holding my badge over me as a way to get me back into the fold and his life. I'd hated him for manipulating me—using his position as the department's psychologist to pull me back to my place in the community—but if he hadn't done it, we wouldn't have solved the case and I wouldn't have stopped the Order. Since then I'd forgiven him for being pushy. I'd been doing a lot of forgiving lately.

"Took you long enough," a middle-aged balding guy said. He'd given me lip the first time, we'd met, too.

"Don't be a dick," Avery snapped as he left the room. She ushered us over to her computer terminal.

"I got through analyzing the footage near Park Street. It doesn't make sense."

"Show me," I said and leaned over her shoulder, waiting for her to cue up the footage.

I watched as a steady stream of people came out of the inbound section of the station and I spotted Carly among them. "There's our girl."

"Keep a close eye on her," Avery said.

Like I wasn't planning on it already. I was about to ask Avery what about the footage didn't make sense when all of a sudden, in the middle of the group of people, Carly simply vanished. No one around her seemed to notice that a little girl who'd been there one minute was now just *gone*. "What just happened?"

"Could the footage have been magically corrupted?" Jacquie posed.

It wasn't out of the realm of possibility, but Avery shook her head. "I went over the footage with every program I could think of and tested it with the standard magic. The only thing off about what we had just watched is that a little girl disappeared and no one even noticed."

"I know there was magic present. I felt it, smelled it. Whoever took Carly was powerful and exerted a lot of energy to keep everyone around them from noticing what was happening," I said.

"Can you rewind and slow it down?" Jacquie peered over Avery's other shoulder.

"What did you see?" I asked as Avery rewound the video and hit play at half speed.

"Maybe it's nothing but ... wait there, the woman standing next to Carly disappears at the same time."

I stared at the screen, not seeing what my partner had. Avery hadn't picked up on it either. She replayed it at an even slower speed. Instead of focusing on Carly this time, I trained my gaze on the female figure to her right. Sure enough, just before Carly vanished, the woman bumped into the little girl and disappeared entirely.

"Well, shit."

"I can't believe I missed that," Avery muttered. She clasped her hands in front of her and stared at the screen. "I don't think there's much else I can do. I feel kind of useless."

I patted her shoulder. "You aren't useless and I missed it, too. This is good work. Now we know that we're just going to have to chase down that magical signature a different way. At least we have some sort of a description to work from." I noted from the video the woman had been in dark jeans, a black tank top and sported a long dark brown braid. Too bad she had never turned toward the camera though.

I had an inkling of who might be behind Carly's abduction or rather *what could be*. Whisperers had the ability to turn themselves invisible and if I had to guess, powerful ones could do the same to those around them. Motive was another question altogether though. I checked the time and took a step toward the door and addressed Jacquie. "We should head out. See if the parents have come up with that list we asked for."

"You're going to find her, right?" Avery's voice was soft.

"We're going to try like hell," I answered. After a pause, I added, "Can you send a copy of the footage to my phone?"

"Sure. Just give me a few minutes."

Jacquie waited until we were back on the first floor before stepping in front of me to bar my path. "You know what we're dealing with, don't you?"

"I don't know what you mean," I answered quietly.

"You got a look of recognition when you saw the woman disappear. Tell me what we're up against. I may not be magical, but I can still fight the bad guys."

"A Whisperer. Their magic turns against them making them invisible whenever they want to be," I explained. "I've only met one of them before, Kayla."

"Unless she's changed her look recently, I don't think she's our culprit."

"No, but she can't be the only Whisperer out there," I answered. Admittedly, I had no idea whether Kayla would know how to find our mystery woman or if Whisperers even hung out together. Still it was definitely worth pursuing at this point, I'd take any lead I could get.

"And you know how to get in touch with her?" Jacquie prompted.

Actually, I hadn't seen Kayla in a few months. At least not since she helped track down a missing gargoyle. Even then, Kayla had just sort of appeared when I needed her. Either that or she was sent by Desmond to check up on me. It wasn't like I had a phone number for her either and mentally noted I should remedy that. "I'll take care of it."

I checked the time again. It was almost dark. Carly had been missing going on six hours. Our window of opportunity to have a positive outcome was rapidly shrinking. Before Jacquie could say anything else, my phone buzzed with an incoming call from J.T. "One second," I said, turned my back to my partner and answered the call. "Hey."

"Hey, so I know we were having dinner tonight," he began.

"I'm late, aren't I?" I groaned.

"No. I need to reschedule. Just got called in for a double shift at work. I'm sorry."

A part of me was annoyed he was rescheduling on me so last minute. Still, I knew we both had demanding jobs which meant we could be called in at a moment's notice. I could feel the pull of the case starting to take over already, bringing with it tunnel vision and little time for romance. "It's fine," I replied.

"Ezri, I know we haven't had a lot of time together lately," J.T. started.

"We'll figure it out. Go be a hero," I answered before ending the call. I spun back around and told Jacquie, "I'll let you know what I get from Kayla."

"I need to head to the station. Mr. and Mrs. Ramirez have the list of people in Carly's life. I'll start going over it, so drop me on your way."

"Here's hoping one of us finds something useable," I muttered. Jacquie started for the door and I followed after her. "I'm going to check with Desmond and see if he knows where I might find Kayla."

As we weaved through rush-hour traffic, my mind drifted to what I knew about Whisperers. Having only met the one, it was limited. Her magic had backfired on her and now my resident punk informant could turn invisible whenever she pleased. She could even move through solid matter like it wasn't there. Which would be useful if one wanted to commit criminal acts.

"You sure Desmond will know where to find Kayla?" Jacquie posed, pulling me from my mental cataloguing.

"Considering he sic'd her on me three months ago, I'm hoping so. Carly doesn't have time for us to go chasing ghosts all over town," I answered.

"No, she doesn't."

"What brought Troy by earlier?" I asked, hoping the change in topic to her nephew would give my mind a chance to reset its focus.

"It's nothing," Jacquie said through pursed lips.

I'd hit a nerve. I had thought we were moving away from being so guarded. "It's just he seemed upset. In all the time we've been partners, he's never shown up while you were at work," I noted.

"Ezri, drop it."

I sat there, staring at my partner's reflection in the rearview mirror, my mouth hanging open. I knew better than to push her now so I shut up. The rest of the car ride turned into an awkward game of trading side glances as we hit every damn red light along the way.

We parted ways silently in the parking lot and I darted up to the second floor, tracing the now-familiar path to Desmond's office. I could see a thin line of light beneath the door and I heard my cousin's voice. I paused, my hand raised to knock much like I had done the first time our paths had crossed at work, when I heard footsteps from within. Not wanting to look like an idiot, I lowered my hand and took a step back.

The door opened and a stocky man in a windbreaker shuffled out. I didn't recognize him, but Desmond was responsible for the mental health of most of the force, not just my division. Desmond stuck his head out into the hallway and spotted me.

"I'm guessing this isn't a social call. Come in."

Crossing the threshold, I was flooded with memories of the first time we'd shared the space together. I'd lashed out—verbally and magically—and he'd just taken it. He'd had to remind me that I wasn't the only person who'd felt the loss of my mother a decade ago. He'd carried a burden no teenager should have been forced to keep.

"I need to find Kayla," I said without preamble.

He made a show of looking around his office. "She's not here."

"*Obviously*. But, since you were the one who assigned her to be my shadow during the Taggart case, I assumed you knew how to find her.'"

"Aren't you supposed to be the detective in the family, Ez?" He quipped with a smirk and a laugh.

"Cut the snarky shit, Desmond. I'm trying to find a missing kid. Someone with magic took her. All signs point to a Whisperer and Kayla's the only one I know."

"Okay, I'm sorry," he said, his face going serious as he reached for his phone. He tapped the screen a few times and I heard the telltale ping of a message being sent. "I just texted you her number. I'm pretty sure she said she was going to see Kevin today."

Kevin Ellery, as in the gargoyle she'd helped me

track down. The one she'd been in love with and who'd taken the fall for murdering five people.

SEVEN

I leaned against the hood of my car in the visitor lot of the prison, tracking every person who moved through the side door. Not that Kayla would be hard to spot if she were corporeal with her punk-rock look, but my nerves were wound tight. I didn't want to miss her. Finally, after watching nearly two dozen people come and go, the door opened and a black-clad young woman with a purple pixie cut emerged.

"How is he?" I called, hoping to draw her attention.

She turned at the sound of my voice and a look of surprise washed over her face. I was clearly not who she had expected to see. Kayla strode toward me, her hands in the pockets of her skirt. "What are you doing here?"

"Looking for you. Please get in," I replied and gestured to the passenger seat.

She turned translucent, passing through the door and became solid again once inside. Once I settled behind the wheel, I turned to face her. "Really, how is Kevin holding up?"

Kayla sighed and looked at her hands. "He tries to keep to himself, but people still talk shit about him. He's been beaten up a lot. Without his magic, he's not as strong as he used to be."

"I'm sorry," I said.

"You did what you had to do. He's not mad about that. I think a part of him is relieved to be able to clear his conscience. At least Kev doesn't have to see *him*."

I didn't need to ask her who she meant. Jamison Taggart had been decorated FBI until he tried to kill me and unleash evil druids on the city. Now he was rotting behind bars where he belonged. Still, I hadn't come out of our encounter unscathed. The magic he'd used to encase Kevin in stone and control him now resided in me. The tiny nugget of dark magic—a literal rock in my stomach—throbbed at the mere thought of him. I pressed a hand to my ribs reflexively, even though everything felt like it should. I swallowed to get myself under control. I'd sought out Kayla for a reason. "I need your help. I'm working a missing person's case, a little girl from the community named Carly Ramirez."

"I don't think I know her," Kayla answered.

"That's not why I need you." I pulled out my phone and hit play on the video from Avery. "She's a Whisperer, isn't she?"

Kayla snatched the phone from me and rewound the footage. "I mean, maybe. I couldn't do that, but I've heard of people. They have more power, can even expand their invisibility field to include other people and objects."

"Any of those people have names?" I prodded.

"It's not like we all hang out together," Kayla muttered, trailing off like she wanted to say more.

"There's something you're not saying. Please, a little girl's life depends on it. The magic I sensed was powerful, but already fading."

"Can't you like follow it? Isn't that your thing?" She asked.

"If I went back now, I don't know if I could trace it beyond the general area Carly was taken from. It doesn't help that they literally disappeared in a crowd. Besides Carly didn't put up a fight so it's not like I could track her magic, either. So please, if you know anything ... you need to tell me."

Kayla chewed her lip. "I might know someone that might know who it is. You don't want to deal with him though. He's dangerous."

"I'm the freaking Savior, remember. I'm pretty sure I'm scarier." I patted my hip holster. "Besides,

I'm a cop. That tends to carry a little extra weight, too."

"You don't know this guy. I'm not even sure if he's still around. I'd have to go looking. Anyways like you said, you're running against a clock."

"So, go find him," I said, my tone sharper than I had intended. I took the phone back and sent a quick text. "I just sent you my number. Let me know the second you find him. I don't care if it's the middle of the night."

"I'll try," she answered, this time staying solid and opening the passenger side door.

I watched her walk through the maze of parked cars in the lot until she vanished from my line of sight. I leaned on the steering wheel and blew out a slow breath trying to shake out some of the anxious energy building up. Exerting a little will, I let the sweet scent of my magic fill the car. I breathed it in and let it calm me down. I had to believe we were going to find Carly—alive and safe—because the alternative wasn't an option.

EIGHT

By the time I got back to the precinct, the sun had already sunk below the horizon. Despite the warm summer air, I shivered at the thought of Carly out there with strangers doing who knew what to her. I settled at my desk, noting that Jacquie was bent over a handwritten list of names and addresses.

"What did you find out?" She asked, glancing up at the sound of my chair squeaking under my weight.

"Nothing yet. But Kayla will keep me updated. You have any luck?"

She shook her head, setting aside the list. "No. So far, I've run background checks on everyone. They've all come back clean. We don't have the manpower right now to go knocking on doors and bring everyone in to confirm alibis."

"Let me see the list." I held out my hand and she

passed it over. I took a picture and sent Desmond a text, 'How many of these names crossover with Authority membership?'.

His response came almost immediately. "All of them except the school teachers."

"I have an idea. Everyone, but the teachers on this list are members of the Authority. I can put word out to the Council, bring them all in tomorrow morning. We talk to them there."

"Where are the police detectives looking for my son?" A man yelled, effectively stalling our discussion.

I turned to find a tall, imposing man berating the desk sergeant. The man had close cropped dark curls and a flat nose framed by thin wire-rim glasses. His swarthy complexion was ashen. One of the uniforms near the front desk moved to intercept him, but I had a feeling I was his intended target.

"Your Adrian's father?" I said, standing and moving to put myself in the man's path.

"Yes. Are you the detective who is looking for him?" He spoke with a heavy accent, possibly from the Caribbean or Haiti.

"I am. Please, why don't you come with me and we can talk in private."

He nodded, taking shallow breaths as I led him to one of the interview rooms. I eased the door shut before setting my pen and pad on the table between us. "Do you mind if I ask how you found out Adrian is missing?"

"My ex-wife, she called my phone. She said she was trying to make sure it still worked, because the police would want to talk to me." He leaned on his arms so there was very little air between us. "I did not hurt my son and I do not appreciate the police thinking I did."

"Sir, I can assure you I didn't think you took him. Although, when there's one parent out of the picture, we do need to look into the relationship. If you're still in touch with your son then you might know something about where he went, even if you don't think you do. Now, Belladonna mentioned Adrian had been looking into your side of the family recently ... Your heritage."

"What's that supposed to mean?" He spat.

Thankfully the interview rooms weren't equipped with audio and video. So, it was a little safer to speak candidly. "Your family's magic. From what I understand, that's part of the reason you and Belladonna split up. Cultural differences on how to raise your son."

He leaned back with arms crossed over his chest. "And what do you know about any magic?"

I smiled. "Forgive me for not introducing myself. I'm Ezri Trenton."

He stared blankly at me. "Is that supposed to mean something to me?"

Well, shit. I guess my family name didn't mean much if you didn't believe in the Western way magic was used. "You heard about the serial murders from a few months ago right?"

"It was all over the news."

"That was an effort by some very bad people to make things even worse by raising the spirits of long-dead druids. My ancestors prophesized that I'd be the one to stop them. And I did."

"I see. So, you have great magic."

"Yeah. I do. I want to use it to find your son, but I need you to help me understand what he was looking into. The more I know about his mindset before he disappeared, the better chance I have of finding him."

"Our people believe it is a family's duty to teach our children how to use their gifts. Belladonna did not want to do that. She believed in the Western way. Sending our boy away to learn from strangers."

I opened my mouth to tell him that she'd been training him herself, but realized it would only make things worse. "And he reached out recently to reconnect with your side of the family. Right?"

"Yes."

"Did he ask you about anything specific? Do you or your relatives have any particular skills that a teenage boy might find useful or interesting? I know he has healing from his mother's side of the bloodline."

Adrian's father looked away; his arms still crossed over his chest. His lips pressed into a firm line and he stayed silent. Everything about his body language screamed avoidance. He had information that he either thought made him look guilty or cast his family in a bad light. I didn't care which column it fell into. I needed to know. "Look, it might reflect negatively on you right now. But I swear it will help."

"You are young, even for a savior. There is much you do not know."

"You're right. So, help me understand what I don't know."

He glanced around the room, as if he didn't believe we were safe from prying ears. "My family's gifts lay with communing with the dead. Nothing like raising it or anything like that. That's disrespectful to their spirits. What you described we would never do."

I jotted down notes to remind myself to research anything I could about magic dealing with the dead. "Is there anyone Adrian would have wanted to try to commune with if he tapped into that part of his lineage?" I held up a hand to stop him from interrupting or arguing with me. "I understand you wouldn't do that. He's a fifteen-year-old kid, not exactly the most logical of people. Trust me, I used to be one."

"No. He did not want to commune with anyone specific. But he did want to know if our gifts ran in

African families predominantly. He also wanted to know if they were more prone to having the sight.'

"The sight? Like premonitions and prophecies?" I prompted.

"Yes."

"And do they? Run in the African community?" I felt like such an idiot for having to ask him.

"Some families, yes. Also, the Hispanic communities, especially those from South America. But we do not have any roots there."

"I know it doesn't feel like it, but this is really helpful," I said. "Just out of curiosity, in families that do have these skills, does it usually show up in one sex over the other?"

"Was your mother's magic not stronger than your father's?" He replied.

"So, magic still obeys certain rules of being passed through the maternal line. Got it." A knock on the door disrupted the flow of our conversation. Before I could answer it, the door opened and Jacquie stepped into the room. "I need to speak with you."

I turned to Adrian's father. "Excuse me for just a minute." I pushed over my pad and pen. "Could you give me your contact information and a list of your whereabouts for the last four days?'

"So, I am still a suspect," he huffed.

"We just need to exclude you. We did the same with your ex-wife," I said, hoping that since

Belladonna had been treated the same way—even as the custodial parent—he'd lower his hostility.

"Very well," he grumbled.

I followed Jacquie out of the room and down a short hallway. "What's wrong?" I asked.

"The techs got finished analyzing the footage from South Station. You need to see it."

My stomach dropped, acid burned the back of my throat and my mind played through the two most likely scenarios. *His father had in fact taken him or our mystery Whisperer was responsible for his abduction, too.* Wordlessly, I trailed my partner back to the bullpen. I pulled a chair over to her desk and she hit play on the video. I spotted Adrian coming around the corner from the stairs, phone still in hand. He glanced at it—maybe checking the time—and started through the corridor to the escalators up to the bus terminals. He took the escalator up two at a time and disappeared from the camera's view.

"Where'd he go?"

"He seems to have found a camera blind spot. Just wait," Jacquie answered.

I kept watching and spotted a kid matching Adrian's general description wearing a hoodie and baseball hat coming down from the bus terminal. He tossed his phone in the trash, but produced another phone from his sweatshirt pocket. He tapped it, held it to his ear for thirty seconds and then ended the call. I watched him stroll out of the camera's range like he didn't have a care in the world.

We didn't know that his father wasn't involved, but it looked increasingly like Adrian had left of his own accord. His disappearing act had been planned. We needed access to his computer. I was also beginning to wonder if his disappearance and Carly's abduction were more interrelated than I'd initially thought.

"Well that's not what I was expecting," I finally said.

"Nope. We have no way of knowing who he called without the second phone."

"So, we subpoena both parents' phone records and see if either of them received a call. We know what time he made it. If it wasn't one of them, at least we've ruled out their involvement." I pushed myself around to my own desk, ready to start the process of getting Belladonna and her ex-husband's phone records when my own phone rang in my pocket. The 'non-specific' ringtone had me checking the display to see a number flash across the screen identified as 'Maybe: Kayla.'

"Hey, I wasn't expecting you to call so soon," I said.

"His name is Jonathan. He runs a place that caters to our people called Notre Dame out near BU." Her voice shook when she mentioned her source's name. It seemed like he really scared her.

"Thank you. Really. I owe you one."

"Just try not to get killed, okay? You're not a totally sucky Savior after all and I kind of want you still breathing."

I'd missed her brand of snark. Her warning wasn't lost on me. Whoever this Jonathan was, I needed to be on my guard.

JUNE 20, 2017

NINE

My car's clock read just after midnight—thanks to the club not opening until 11:00—when I finally found a spot half a block up from where my GPS said Notre Dame was supposed to be. I'd lived not far from here for years and I'd never heard of it. Then again, if they catered to the magical community, I'd have no reason for it to have been on my radar before now. I sat in the driver seat debating whether to go in with my gun. It would give me an added layer of protection, but I didn't know what I was walking into. Besides with other magically inclined people inside, I could easily lose the advantage. I stowed it in the glove compartment, but kept my badge clipped to my belt.

"Line forms over there, sweetheart," a pale-skinned, bald, and thickly muscled bouncer said. He pointed to the line snaking down the block and around the corner of the building.

"I'm a VIP," I said and flashed my badge.

He glared at me, but didn't bar my entrance. I stepped into the dim entryway to the bar and took the moment while my eyes adjusted to clear my palette. I wasn't sure I'd be able to find the Whisperer in a crowd of swirling magical signatures, but I was damn well going to try. Pulsing basslines thrummed through the floor and up my legs as I made my way further inside.

It turned out Notre Dame was an odd mix of nightclub and restaurant. Booths lined the east wall with a wood-topped bar running opposite it. Smack in the middle was a dance floor, complete with a DJ and the origin of the heavy bass. I scanned the throng of throbbing bodies and took a deep breath. I coughed as the overlapping signatures hit me. I moved to the bar and took shallow breaths to center myself. I hadn't sensed anything remotely like brackish water.

"You need some help, darling?" A man with a thick Boston accent asked from behind the bar.

"Depends on who's asking, *honey*?" I answered.

"Touchy." He glanced down at my waist and back up. "You don't look old enough to be a cop."

I leaned my elbows on the bar. "Detective. I'm looking for the owner. Know where I might find him?"

He laughed, flashing two rows of perfectly straight teeth. "You found him."

"I wasn't expecting the owner to be tending bar."

"I'm a man of many talents." He reached behind himself in a move that shouldn't have been possible given where he was standing and pulled a glass off the shelf. Pouring something that smelled strongly of mint in before sliding it to me. "Now, what can I do for you, Detective ..."

"Trenton," I supplied ignoring the drink.

"Detective Trenton." He leaned on his forearms, closing the distance between us with what he probably thought was a flirty smile. "You wouldn't happen to be that Savior everyone was going on about a couple months back."

I arched a brow. "And what if I was?"

"Well, I'd tell you that I don't like cops in my bar ... especially ones who bring out the crazies."

"Well, I heard you're the man to see if I'm looking for magical folks who aren't exactly on the right side of the law."

"Did you now? And who might have put that little notion in your head?"

"Someone I trust." I gestured to the dance floor. "I'm guessing you don't have just upstanding Authority-abiding citizens in your fine establishment. I'm looking for a Whisperer."

"Can't help you," he said, his flirtatious smile vanished.

"Look, I don't care if you don't like me. I've got a missing ten-year-old girl and time isn't on her side. So, how about you be a decent human being and help me out."

"Sorry about your missing kid, Detective. I can't help you. Now, I'm going to have to ask you to leave and I'd prefer you didn't make a scene."

I glanced over my shoulder to see the burly bouncer watching me. I felt it in my bones that Jonathan knew something about who took Carly. I needed to find a way to convince him to talk to me. As inconspicuously as I could, I let the power around me build. I focused on Jonathan's face, putting out into the world that I needed him to tell the truth. My magic bumped up against some sort of barrier and I saw his neck muscles tighten. I let the spell drop.

"Okay, you got it," I said, stepping back from the bar and gesturing toward the front entrance. "But I hope you can live with your conscience if something bad happens to that little girl."

He tapped his chest with one hand. "Don't you worry about my conscience, Savior."

As I moved toward the door I'd come through, I caught the heavy scent of lemons coming from behind the bar. It was an almost visible shimmer of charcoal that protectively wrapped itself around the bartender like a cloak. *What is he hiding?*

TEN

I retreated back to my apartment, though I knew I wouldn't be sleeping. Too much rattled around in my head. Questions needing answers that I didn't have and feared would come too late. My place wasn't much—a one bedroom—but it suited me just fine. It wasn't like J.T. and I were in a place where we were thinking about moving in together. As a bonus, the neighbors didn't seem to notice my odd hours or random scents of magic.

Locking my gun into the lockbox in my bedroom, I spotted the boxes of magical texts my mother had squirreled away before her death. They were a mix of witchcraft history from the area and reference materials on magical creatures. They'd come in handy before and maybe they could again. I dragged the box containing the general history of the area into the living room and turned on my coffee pot.

As I waited for the coffee to brew, a sense of sadness washed over me. The books brought up memories of my mom and the pentacle that hung beneath my sandalwood charm thrummed warm against my skin. It traced back to the matriarchs of our family who lived during the Witch Trials. It contained a small amount of power from every woman who'd ever worn it through the centuries, including my mother. Three months ago, I'd been able to commune with that part of her contained within the necklace. It was almost like she'd been there with me until she'd sacrificed her magic for me —the second time she'd done something to ensure I was safe—and I hadn't been able to feel her presence since.

"I really wish you were here, Mom," I sighed, the fingertips of my right hand brushing against the necklace. The metal turned white hot against my skin and I pulled my hand away, sticking it in my mouth to suck away the pain. I expected to feel a blister on the pad of my finger or at the very least residual warmth, but the skin was unmarked.

"Forgive me, I did not mean to cause you pain or frighten you," an unfamiliar voice said.

I jumped at the sound and spun around to see a red-haired woman in late seventeenth century clothing standing in my kitchen. She bore the same family resemblance that Desmond did, but I knew she wasn't his ancestor.

"Theodora," I replied.

"Hello dear." She stepped closer and placed a hand on my shoulder. "I know I am not your mother, but I felt I could be of some comfort."

Theodora Harrow was the reason I existed. Her blood ran in my veins and with it her magic. "I appreciate the thought, but honestly, I'm not sure you would understand what's going on. No offense.'

"Child, I know more than you think. Have you not yet come to understand that every woman who wore this pendant is a part of your magic? A part of you."

"I know. You're like a piece of Theodora's soul," I said.

"In a manner of speaking, yes. I am her. I possess her memories and knowledge. Much as my sister and your mother did when they appeared to you. I am also aware of what has transpired."

"Don't take this the wrong way. If I know my history right, the cultures I'm dealing with weren't exactly around or even welcome in the area when you were living."

Theodora reached up and patted my cheek like I was a small child. "My dear, you forget I lived beyond the time of my sister. However, you are on the right path learning about the customs of other practitioners. I do wonder if your situation would have been changed had we welcomed their practices into our ranks rather than keeping ourselves separate. We were not without our own prejudices."

"Things are more diverse these days," I commented.

"Perhaps. But be wary of the darkness. You may have halted its progress, but it still remains ... working against you at every turn." She paced the length of my tiny kitchen. "Promise me one thing as you continue on this journey."

"I'm not the best with promises, but I'll try."

"Do not try to fix everything on your own. You are stronger when you have a force behind you."

I smiled. "Believe me, I'm trying with that one." Being a team player didn't exactly come naturally to me.

"You should rest while you are able, my dear. The battle ahead is long and you will need all of your strength."

"I'll sleep when I'm dead," I muttered, reaching for the coffee pot that should have been done percolating. I blinked dazedly at the empty pot. *I swear I filled that up.* "Theodora, did you ..." I trailed off, realizing I now stood alone in my kitchen.

Maybe she was right. I glanced at the books sprawled on the table in the living room and retreated to my bedroom, hoping sleep would bring clarity.

ELEVEN

I stood in the spot where Carly had vanished, surrounded by empty streets. Not a soul moved around me. The sky was pitch black and from within that eerie darkness a presence loomed. One I'd encountered before. The blackness resolved into Taggart dressed in a black suit, complete with skinny tie. The nauseating scent of his magic wafted from him and closed in on me.

"You're not going to find her," he said, that smarmy grin on his angular face.

"I'm pretty sure you don't get to have an opinion," I retorted.

He laughed throwing his head back in true villain fashion. "You don't think you won, do you? You only delayed us. But you're never going to stop us. We will just keep coming after you. After the children you claim to protect." Taggart grabbed the front of my *shirt and slammed one fist into my rib cage, winding me. "Don't you forget ... Savior, I'm always with you."*

I sat up, cold sweat covering my body and matting my hair to my forehead. I fought to catch my breath, reminding myself it was just a dream. There was no way Taggart had taken Carly. He was behind bars. I pressed my hand to the spot he'd punched in the dream and panic set in. The skin and muscle felt rock hard. I peeled the fabric of my shirt away and felt the color drain from my face at the sight of slate grey stone covering my torso in the early morning dimness. The garlic stench of his magic filled my nostrils, making my eyes water and my stomach contents churn.

"He can't hurt you," I wheezed, scrambling out of bed to the bathroom to take a better look.

My breathing remained ragged as the hardness and stone were not a figment of my imagination. I gulped down air to try and get myself under control. He would not win. I summoned my own power, letting it envelop me, binding tight around my body like armor. The dark magic receded and my heartrate slowed. I splashed cool water on my face, warding off the nightmare and caught sight of the clock on the wall. It was almost five in the morning. I'd managed four hours of sleep.

"Good enough," I told my reflection and set about getting dressed. *Time to get back to the case.*

After making a much-needed stop for coffee up

the road, I made my way back to the precinct. It was just empty enough to let me caffeinate in peace and sort through the details of the case in my mind. Dark magic was definitely in play and I knew Jonathan was hiding something. Still, he wasn't going to talk to me as the Savior. He clearly didn't like cops or the fact I'd been in his space. Although, maybe that was the way in. One search later and I had my ammunition. He couldn't keep serving customers with an expired liquor license.

"Why do you look like you're about to do something questionable?" Jacquie asked, sitting down across from me.

"Kayla gave me a name of someone who might know our mystery kidnapper. I paid him a visit last night, but he wasn't very chatty. Turns out his liquor license expired last month and he hasn't renewed it yet," I explained.

"And you think shutting him down will make him talk?" She didn't sound convinced.

"It's worth a try." I noticed dark circles beneath her eyes and the pallor of her skin suggested she hadn't slept much either. "What do you say we pay him a visit?"

"You think he's still there?"

"Given that he's got ways to skirt the noise ordinances, I'd say he's still there. Besides, it's a little too early to gather folks at headquarters to see if any of them know anything about Carly's disappearance."

Jacquie smiled. "What the hell. Let's go rattle this guy's cage."

WE PULLED up in front of Notre Dame just before six o'clock. The sun was still making its morning ascent over the nearby buildings. The bouncer from the night before was nowhere to be seen. I could still hear the faint pulsing of the sound system filtering out of the partially open front door. I pulled the door open and strode in like I owned the place.

Jonathan leaned against the far end of the bar, swirling something clear in a shot glass. He looked up at the sound of my footsteps and let out an audible growl.

"I thought I told you to get out of my bar."

I plastered on a sugary smile. "You did. So, I came back with a friend. This is my partner, Detective DeWitt. I wanted a witness here when I gave you this," I said and slid the notice shutting him down across the bar.

He picked it up. "This is bullshit."

I gestured to the license behind the bar. "Your license expired last month. City records don't show any renewal pending. So you aren't legally able to serve alcohol."

He stalked over to our end of the bar, a snarl on his lips. "You are a little—" he started.

"I'd be careful what you say to my partner. She'll be more than happy to kick your ass," Jacquie quipped.

I leaned in close. "Now that I've got your attention, why don't you tell me what you know about the person we're looking for?" He glanced toward Jacquie. "Oh, she knows all about who and what I am. So, feel free to speak openly."

"Say I do know something. What's in it for me?"

"We might be a little slow filing anything more official. Possibly give you the time to get yourself back up to code and maybe we let you keep operating while that happens," I answered.

His gaze narrowed as he considered my offer. "Fine. You said your kid was snatched by a Whisperer, right?"

"I said I had a missing girl. I never said she was taken by a Whisperer," I answered.

"Fine, I may have heard chatter about some kid that got snatched."

"And did that chatter include the name of the kidnapper?" Jacquie interjected.

His gaze flitted between us as he considered whether to answer Jacquie's question. After a tense minute or two, he said, "Lola Cox. She's a Whisperer, but she's even less tolerant of police than I am."

I brought up the video footage on my phone and paused it right before Carly vanished. "Is this her?"

He laughed. "Savior, I may be good, but even I can't ID her from the back of her head."

"Does she have any identifying marks?" I pressed.

He tapped the top of his hand. "She's got a tattoo on her left hand. Some weird Celtic thing."

"If you aren't going to be more descriptive, I'm afraid we're going to have to say you were uncooperative and keep you shut down," I said.

"Fine, it's a triple spiral with a scythe. I never understood what she liked about it."

It wasn't a tattoo, more like a brand. The trademark sign of a member of the Order of Samael. *Is that what Theodora meant about the darkness?* "I'm guessing you know where we can find Ms. Cox?"

"She comes in sometimes. Usually middle of the week."

I slid my card to him. "You call me the next time she shows up. You breathe a word of why we're looking for her or that we're coming ... I'll arrest you for obstruction and anything else I can think of. Got it?"

He pocketed the card. "Sure, Savior. Now, get the hell out of my bar."

"See you around, Johnny," I said with a wave and led the way back to the car. At least now we had a name.

I slid into the passenger seat just as the radio in the center console crackled to life. "All units, reports of an abduction reported near Copley Square. Adolescent female."

Jacquie and I shared a look. "Something tells me that isn't a coincidence," I said.

Jacquie picked up the radio. "Unit fifty-seven responding."

I held my breath as she put the car in reverse, flipped on the sirens and pulled an illegal U-turn to head back downtown.

TWELVE

"The tattoo he mentioned. It's the same one Taggart had, right?" Jacquie asked as she weaved between cars heading to Boylston Street.

"Yeah. I didn't notice it in the footage, but that doesn't mean much. She can turn herself basically invisible. And from what Kayla said, she's strong enough to extend her invisibility field to other people. It can't be hard to cover up the brand."

Jacquie opened her mouth to speak when her cell phone rang through the car's Bluetooth. It displayed Troy's face and name. She reached to decline the call.

"No, it's fine. Answer it," I said.

"Are you sure?"

"Yeah."

She hit 'Accept' and said, "Troy, I'm busy right now."

"Aunt Jacquie, she's gone," he said, his pubescent voice cracking.

"Who's gone?"

"Neveah. She was there one minute and then some lady bumped into her and she was gone."

"Where are you right now?" Jacquie's tone took on an edge of panic and her voice modulated a step higher.

"Harvard Square. I know we aren't supposed to be out this early, but Neveah wanted to go for a walk," Troy answered.

"Don't move a muscle, you hear me? We're coming to you," Jacquie said. She tapped the screen and brought up GPS tracking on Troy's location.

"What about the abduction up at Copley?" I asked.

"Radio in that we need someone else to take the call," she said, not taking her eyes from the road as she slammed her foot on the gas pedal.

I picked up the radio. "Unit fifty-seven to dispatch, cancel that responding."

"Confirm, you said you are no longer responding, unit fifty-seven?" The dispatcher crackled over the connection.

"Correct, dispatch. Send closer units."

"Understood."

Bailing on a call wasn't like Jacquie. In fact, she'd been acting oddly since this case started. I'd chalked it up to the stress at home from having the kids go back to living with their mom. *Is it something else?*

The GPS map zoomed in as we drew close to Troy's location. Thankfully, given the early hour very few people populated the streets. We slid to a stop just across from the Harvard Coop. I scrambled to catch up to Jacquie as she bolted from the car, wrapping her nephew in a tight embrace.

"Are you okay?" She asked him, barely giving him space to breathe.

"Jacquie, let him catch his breath," I said, while looking around the spot. In a few hours it would be bustling with people. It would have been easier to take Neveah in a crowd. Carly's abduction proved that already.

"Troy, you said a woman bumped into your sister and they both disappeared?" I asked.

"Yes. I'm so sorry, Aunt Jacquie. I know I'm supposed to protect her." Troy was on the verge of tears and he looked far younger than his thirteen years.

"Don't you dare think this was your fault," Jacquie said sternly, pulling him in for another hug.

I didn't doubt that Troy called Jacquie as soon as his sister had vanished. That meant we were operating in the best window possible for me to trace the kidnapper's signature—assuming it was the same person behind Carly's disappearance—and so I took a step away from nephew and aunt. I reached out with all of my magical senses. The spot about two feet to Troy's right flared to life with the hazy outline of two people moving down the street. The scent of brackish water tickled my nose.

"I've got something," I said and took off.

"What's she doing?" I heard Troy ask from behind me.

"She's got magic just like you and your sister."

If Troy responded to her statement, I didn't hear. Instead, I poured all of my focus into following Lola and Neveah's afterimage until it dead ended three blocks down. I saw skid marks on the pavement, like someone had taken off in a hurry.

"What is it?" Jacquie yelled.

"I lost them." I pointed to the skid marks on the street. "It looks like they got into a car and went that way. I can't track the magic when it's moving that fast. But, it's definitely the same person who took Carly."

"Carly's missing?" Troy gulped.

I rounded on him. "You know Carly Ramirez?"

"Well, only a little. She's more Neveah's friend. Who would want to hurt them?"

I gripped Troy's shoulders and bent down so we were eye level. "I need you to take some deep breaths okay? You're doing good. Do you think you can give us a description of the person who took your sister?"

"Maybe. I didn't really see her that well, but I can try."

"That's all we ask," Jacquie said, ushering him back to our waiting car.

I radioed for back up to secure the scene, hoping someone would be there quick enough that we didn't lose the small advantage we had on Neveah's kidnapping. As Troy climbed in the backseat, I prayed that there was video footage tying Lola to both scenes. If we could positively identify her, we had a better shot at getting the girls back safely.

THIRTEEN

We'd barely gotten inside the front doors when the desk sergeant waved us down. Jacquie pointed to her desk, whispered something in Troy's ear and he slunk off.

"Captain wants you two in her office. She doesn't sound pleased."

"Thanks for the heads up," I said and wound my way through the bullpen to Captain Beech's office.

"Get in here, you two," she boomed.

She rarely took that tone with us and I had a feeling she was pissed about our bailing on the other call. I was going to let Jacquie explain that one.

"You two want to tell me why you cancelled on that abduction call?"

"It was my fault, Captain. My nephew called," Jacquie started.

"DeWitt, I get things are in flux at home, but prioritizing a family matter over an active investigation isn't like you," Captain Beech chastised.

"My niece was taken, Captain," Jacquie said softly.

The captain's posture changed immediately. The hard lines on her face softened. "You're sure?"

"Yes, ma'am."

"Well, we've got a preliminary account of the second victim. It matches the first. She was in a very public place and out of nowhere she vanished," Captain Beech explained.

I wondered why another young girl was out this early in the morning. "We'll start reviewing the available footage right away. We're working on a potential lead," I added.

"You will be looking into the footage. DeWitt is off this case. Give your statement, take your nephew, and go home."

"Captain that's not necessary," Jacquie protested.

"It's not up for discussion."

"I can't do this alone," I said.

"You've got the entire force behind you. And if you're right and the same offender took all three girls, we're going to bring in the feds."

"Captain, we can manage without them," I balked.

"Trenton, I know we are a little gun-shy after what happened with Taggart, but he was an outlier. We need to put aside our feelings to bring these girls home safely."

She said 'we' even though I knew she meant me. Being stabbed and left for dead tends to make anyone a little bristly when it comes to working with the people who harbored your would-be murderer. Still the captain was right. Getting the girls home had to be my top priority. Just because Jacquie couldn't investigate these disappearances didn't mean she couldn't still dig into Adrian's case. I turned to Jacquie. "Come on, I'll take yours and Troy's statements."

Jacquie's face turned into a calm mask, even though I knew she was raging inside. I led her to my desk and leaned in close. "You take Adrian's case. Keep digging into that. We still don't know if it's connected to the girls. I promise, I'll let you know the second we find anything."

"I'm holding you to that," she hissed.

"Aunt Jacquie, what happens now?" Troy asked from his spot across the way.

"You're going to tell Ezri everything that happened," she answered. She looked at me. "I need to call Denise and let her know what happened."

I motioned for Troy to come sit by me as Jacquie stepped away to make her call. Troy slumped in his chair, gaze cast at his feet. I could see remnants of the tears he'd wiped away from his cheeks.

"Does Aunt Jacquie need to be here or something?" He mumbled.

"You aren't under arrest. You're just giving a statement. We can wait for her or your mom if you'd feel more comfortable," I answered.

He glanced in the direction Jacquie had gone. "No. We don't have to wait."

"Okay. Let's start at the beginning. You guys were out by yourselves pretty early. Do you usually go out before seven?"

"Neveah couldn't sleep. She misses Aunt Jacquie and said she's been having bad dreams since Mom came back. Something about ghosts. I figured she was just being dramatic, but we were just going for a walk so she could calm down," he answered.

"How are things at home now that you're back living with your mom?"

"Okay. She's trying. I don't think Neveah understood that. She's there when we get home from school which is nice, I guess. But ..."

"You got used to how things were with Jacquie."

"Yeah."

"Did you let your mom know you were going out?"

"No. She was still asleep. I didn't want to wake her up."

I pictured her getting the call from Jacquie. A

scramble to check the bedrooms to be sure her children weren't safely tucked in bed. A frantic dash to get down to the station. Troy hadn't done his mother any favors by not letting her know they were leaving.

"Okay. So, you're out for a walk. Did you see anyone following you?"

"No. I don't think so." He scrunched his eyes shut, clearly trying to replay the morning's events in his head. "We passed the coffee place by the T. She wanted to go in and get something to eat. I told her we couldn't, because we didn't have any money. I told her we should go home, because we'd been out long enough. She didn't want to listen. She hates it when I tell her what to do."

"So, what did you do next?" I prompted.

"I grabbed her arm and pulled her back the way we'd come. She yelled at me to let her go. I didn't want people to think I was trying to hurt her so I let go. Then, some white lady just walked down the street, bumped into Neveah and they were gone."

"Troy, this is really important. When she walked down the street, was she facing you? Could you see her face or anything about her at all?"

"Um, she had dark hair. I remember, because it made her look really pale."

"Okay. What about her eye color or any other distinguishing features?" I needed more evidence. Having the same magical signature at both crime scenes wasn't enough for a judge to issue an arrest warrant for Lola Cox.

"She was wearing sunglasses. The kind with the really reflective lenses. She had some weird tattoo on her hand though," he said.

"Tattoo? Can you describe it?"

Instead of answering, he reached over, grabbed my notepad and pen. He scribbled something on a clean page before passing the pad back to me. "Here."

I studied his drawing. *Kid should be an artist.* It was a perfect triple spiral with a scythe in the center. "You're sure that's what you saw?"

"Yeah. It kind of felt familiar, but I don't know why," he answered.

I was about to explain the significance when raised voices echoed from the front of the building. Jacquie stormed in after a thin woman with dark skin and short-cropped hair. I could see bags under her eyes.

"Denise, just slow down," Jacquie barked.

"Where's my baby?" Denise demanded, scanning the sparsely populated bullpen until her eyes landed on her son. "What did you do?"

"He didn't do anything," Jacquie snapped, moving to block her sister-in-law's path.

"Your auntie calls me, tells me your sister is missing. I tell her that can't be right," Denise moaned.

"She was upset. I was just trying to calm her down," Troy said, sitting up.

Denise rounded on Jacquie. "This has something to do with you, doesn't it?"

"Mrs. DeWitt, can we talk privately for a minute? I'm the detective working your daughter's case," I said calmly. I gestured to the same interview room I'd used the day before with Adrian's father. "Please."

Denise stomped off in the direction I'd pointed. When I stepped in the room and eased the door shut, she seemed to have collected herself. "I'm sorry about that," she said, sinking into one of the chairs.

"It's a very emotional time for everyone. I want to assure you that what happened to your daughter isn't related to Jacquie."

"How do you know?" Denise sniffled.

"Because someone with magic took her and Jacquie's bloodline isn't magical."

Denise bristled, her shoulders straightened and she jutted her chin forward. "So, you're saying this is *my* fault?"

"No. I'm just telling you that we believe your daughter's abduction is magic-related. I know your children were only back with you recently, but do you know if they were involved with anything in the community?"

"Involved with what? My kids aren't into anything dangerous or criminal," she responded.

"I meant were they getting training of any kind for their abilities?"

"Oh." Her shoulders relaxed and she laid her hands on the table between us. "I think so. Honestly, I wasn't really involved with it. I haven't used mine in forever. Don't think I'd even remember where to start."

"Troy said that Neveah was friendly with Carly Ramirez. Do you know if they spent a lot of time together?"

"You'd have to ask Jacquie. She knew their friends better than me. Please, just bring my baby home. I just got her and her brother back."

"I'm going to do everything I can," I said, feeling like a broken record.

I needed to get any information I could on our third victim before the FBI swooped in and complicated matters. Confirming the surveillance footage at both new crime scenes was also on the top of my to-do list. I led Denise back to the bullpen where Troy and Jacquie waited.

"Denise should take Troy home. There's nothing else they can do here. I need you to put a list together of everyone in Neveah's life," I said, addressing Jacquie.

"You'll have it on your desk within the hour," she answered, pulling out a piece of paper and pen as she spoke.

Denise shuffled forward and placed a hand on

Troy's shoulder, guiding him away. Jacquie watched them go before turning to me. "I thought you'd want to know; the techs are bringing in Adrian's computer. If there's anything to find, they'll have it soon."

"Good. I'm going to update Avery and then I need to pay an old friend a visit," I said, grabbing my keys.

FOURTEEN

Visiting hours at the prison didn't typically start this early, but my badge was the exception. I waited in a small room with a table and two chairs, a thick metal bar protruding from one side. The door to my right opened and a familiar figure shuffled in—hands and ankles shackled—and sat down across from me.

Life behind bars may have meant a serious lack of hair gel, but it hadn't dulled Jamison Taggart's sharp features or penetrating stare. He did sport several fresh cuts and bruises on his cheeks and knuckles. Apparently, they'd stuck him in the general population. He waited patiently as the guard secured his wrists to the bar on the table. The guard took up a position by the door. I wanted to ask him to wait outside, but I knew prison protocol wouldn't allow it unless I'd been his attorney. I was going to need to get creative.

"I must admit, I wasn't expecting this visit ... Detective and certainly not at such an early hour," Taggart said coolly.

"Believe me, I'd rather be anywhere else but here," I replied.

He leaned forward. "So, what did I do now that requires your presence?"

"I've got three missing girls and evidence that points to someone in your past organization," I said as vaguely as I could.

"Hmm, I don't think that news has made it inside these walls. And in case you missed it, I am no longer affiliated with that particular organization."

I let out a harsh bark of laughter. "Please, we both know being locked up has done nothing to sever those ties. Now, why don't you be a halfway decent human being and tell me where I can find Lola Cox."

"I'm afraid that name doesn't ring a bell. And no, I don't know anything about any abductions."

"Right. You only targeted people over eighteen. What a saint."

"It wasn't personal, Detective," he said.

That part I believed. "Come on, Taggart. You weren't some low-level flunky. You had position and power. I'm betting a lot of things didn't happen without your say-so. Now, why don't you stop being a heartless dick and help me."

"You know, you really ought to work on your interrogation techniques, Detective. You aren't going to establish any sort of rapport by insulting your witness."

God, he's such an ass. "If you help me, I can put in a word about getting you transferred somewhere nicer. Maybe out of the general population," I bartered.

"You don't think I can handle a few thugs? I'm a trained federal agent, little girl," he snarled.

I glanced at the guard who stood at attention, seemingly not following our conversation at all. "You are very lucky we are not alone. Or that comment would have tacked on some extra years to your sentence." My anger at him for dicking me around forced my magic to seep out of every pore, filling the small space with the scent of fresh strawberries. If the guard noticed, he didn't react.

"Temper, temper," Taggart chided with a cluck of his tongue. "I'm telling you the truth. If there is someone out there who is abducting children and they happen to be linked to my former affiliates, it was not on my orders. Still, I would be very concerned if there is a connection. You may have stopped one effort, but that wasn't our only goal."

"You may all be a bunch of sadistic assholes, but I'm going to stop you. It's in my job description after all," I retorted, doing my best to mask the fear bubbling in my gut.

He said nothing in response. I wasn't going to get anything more from him. I'd need to hunt down Lola myself. I pushed the chair back, the legs scraping against the cold concrete floor. "He can go back to his cell now," I told the guard.

"About that transfer?" Taggart said as the guard unshackled him from the table.

I arched a brow at him. "Well, seeing as you didn't give me anything useful, the deal's off," I answered.

The scent of rotten garlic bloomed in the tiny room as Taggart's magic flared. I could feel his intent without him even laying a hand on me. My windpipe constricted just a little, making it harder to breathe. I rasped for air and pushed back with my own power. The dueling scents were nauseating as I tried to fight him off, all the while magically invisible hands clamped harder on my throat. My gaze narrowed as the sweet tang of fruit overtook the rotting spice and my will superimposed his own. I sent him staggering sideways as the guard hauled him toward the door.

I watched them go and breathed a sigh of relief when I was alone. It gave me time to cleanse myself of his disgusting magical touch. I returned to the front of the prison, reclaimed my phone and gun. I had a missed call from Jacquie. Pressing the phone to my ear, I listened to her message.

"Ezri, I hope whatever lead you are chasing pans out, because time is running out."

Reminding me our window was rapidly shrinking wasn't necessary. I was very much aware of it. I owed her an update, but first I needed to pay the third crime scene a visit.

FIFTEEN

Thank God for a modern case management system. I could access the information on the third scene from my car. By the time I pulled up to Newbury Street and stepped onto the sidewalk a block from the scene, I knew everything non-magical about the crime. Twelve-year-old Gabby Freeman had been out walking early with her mother and younger brother when she'd simply vanished.

I wove my way through the late morning pedestrian foot traffic in the area. I darted across Boylston Street, glaring at the Duck Boat driver who barely swerved to avoid hitting me. I spotted the area of the street cordoned off with crime scene tape. A bored looking uniformed officer stood watch.

"Detective Trenton," I said and held up my badge.

"Something I can help you with, Detective?" He asked.

"Letting me look around the scene would be nice. I'm working a pair of similar abductions and we just need to confirm we've got a serial."

"So, they can bring in the big dogs," he huffed.

"Above my pay grade," I replied.

"Ain't that the truth. Sure, take a look around. Not that it's much to look at."

I ducked beneath the tape and took note of the nearby store cameras. "You been here the whole time?"

"Yep. Drew the short straw."

"You happen to know if they already set things in motion to pull the store footage?"

"I think so. You know, I hate cases with kids. Just something about it sets my stomach on edge."

"Me, too. Me, too," I muttered.

Taking a few steps away from the officer, I positioned myself in the direction that Gabby and her family had been traveling. I closed my eyes, once more letting my magical senses overtake my mundane ones. The same signature I'd sensed at Carly and Neveah's scenes was present. I'd almost hoped this case wasn't related, but life never works out like we hope.

"You alright, Detective?" The officer asked, eying me with a concerned look.

"Yeah, fine. Just trying to get a feel for what

might have prompted the abductor to strike so brazenly."

He nodded mutely before turning to shoo away some nosy tourists, pointing at the tape and trying to duck under. Having confirmed we were in fact working a serial kidnapping, I needed to bring the three families together. Troy had already confirmed that Neveah and Carly knew each other. Given their ages, I suspected Gabby might be part of their group. Meaning someone could have targeted them as a group. *But why? Could they be trying to cast some sort of spell that needed three sacrifices? Or were they grooming them for something larger?*

I traced the path back to my car, hit redial on Jacquie's voicemail and waited as the line rang. Jacquie answered on the third ring. "Please tell me you got something useful out of that bastard."

"No luck. I need you to meet me at Headquarters. I'm going to bring in Carly and Gabby's parents too. We're going to figure out why these girls were targeted."

Swallowing back a lump in my throat, I swung by the precinct to grab copies of all three case files. I didn't see any FBI jacketed newcomers yet so maybe Captain Beech hadn't called in the heavy hitters. If I could at least establish a connection between the girls and their routines, I could feed the feds information without risking exposing magic.

If the Order was behind the abductions as Lola's affiliation suggested and Taggart's assertion that they didn't operate without some nefarious motive was true—which given my prior interactions seemed legit —then I needed to sort out what that motive might be. Using someone who could turn invisible to do your dirty work was pretty clever honestly.

I pulled up a map of the city, plotting the location of each abduction site. While they formed a triangle of sorts—you were bound to get that with three data points—it didn't look ominous like the pentagram the Order had used to fuel their resurrection ritual. Still maybe I was missing something that my mother's books could clear up.

My research would have to wait until I could speak with all three families at once. I also needed to warn the rest of the community to keep a closer eye on their children. I pulled up the Ramirez's phone number and keyed it in on my desk phone. The line rang only once before Mr. Ramirez answered,

"Mr. Ramirez, it's Detective Trenton. Are you with your wife right now?"

"Yes. We haven't left the house since yesterday. Has something happened? Did you find Carly?"

"I'm afraid not. But I need you and your wife to meet me at Headquarters in a half an hour."

"Why?"

"Please just trust me. Meet me in a half hour," I reiterated and hung up. Time to introduce myself to Mrs. Freeman. A tired female voice answered on the third ring.

"Is this Melissa Freeman?"

"Yes. Who is this?"

"My name is Detective Ezri Trenton. I'm investigating your daughter's disappearance," I replied, hoping my name would strike a chord in her head so that I wouldn't have to speak the word 'magic' aloud in the precinct.

"You're the Savior," she supplied.

"That's right. Can you and your family meet me at Headquarters in half an hour?"

"Yes. We'll be there."

I'd just gathered the files I needed when I sensed a presence just out of my peripheral vision. I straightened and pivoted slowly to find Kayla. She was standing there completely visible and looking as if she hadn't slept.

"I'm about to head out," I told her, tucking the files under my arm.

"Oh, I was just stopping by to ask if that information was useful."

"Somewhat. Come with me," I replied, ushering her out of the building and to my car. Much like at the prison, she simply faded through the car door before putting on enough mass to fill the passenger seat.

I set the files in the backseat, climbed behind the wheel and headed out of the city. I replayed my interactions with Jonathan from the night before and that morning. She should know that he had seemed overly interested in who'd given me his name.

"So, why does Jonathan not like law enforcement?" I broached.

"They harsh his mellow," Kayla answered in a monotone.

"Okay, cut the shit, Emo girl," I said, adopting a little of her flare for sassy nicknames.

"Excuse me?" She said, her head whipping around to stare at me with wide eyes.

"You heard me. How do you know this guy? What's his deal? When I was there, I sensed a lot of active magic around him, like literally wrapping itself around him."

Kayla tugged at the lower strands of purple spikes behind her ear. "He's a hunchback. I don't mean that in a derogatory way or anything. I mean literally, he was born with a birth defect. He uses magic to make himself appear less scary looking."

"Does the name Lola Cox mean anything to you?" I asked as I veered toward the exit ramp.

"I wish it didn't. Is that who you think is behind the kidnapping?"

"Kidnappings," I corrected. "And that's the name your bartender buddy gave me. Is he wrong to think she might do the Order's dirty work?"

"I didn't know she was involved with the Order. Are you sure?"

"I've got a witness who places their identifying brand on her."

"That must be recent," Kayla commented.

"So, you do know her."

"A long time ago, when this first happened," she gestured to her body. "I sort of fell in with some rough people and Lola took me under her wing, I guess. She showed me the ropes. I haven't seen or spoken to her in years. If she's working for the Order now, they must be paying her a ton of money. That was always Lola's main focus. She always wanted more than she had."

"All good things to know." I took my eyes off the road long enough to catch Kayla's body language change. Her shoulders hunched and her arms wrapped around her torso as if she was trying to protect herself. There was clearly more to the story than she was letting on.

"You know, if this keeps being a thing, you'll have to get a badge of your own," I said, hoping to lighten the mood.

"Huh?" she mumbled absently.

"Well, this is the second case you've helped me on. A few more and we'll have to make you an honorary detective."

"Heh ... yeah." She fell silent again and I decided not to push. She wasn't ready to share whatever was on her mind. Besides I knew what it was like not wanting to open up to people who claimed they gave a damn about you.

The rest of the drive passed quickly and I pulled into the circular drive. Even before I was up the front steps, I could feel the buzz of energy in the place. Not exactly magic, but the nerves of so many people all anticipating the same thing. Kayla trailed behind me as I crossed the threshold and barely avoided being accosted by Mrs. Ramirez.

"What has happened? Why are we all here?" She demanded.

I pointed to the staircase leading to the upper floor. "Upstairs in the council room. I'll explain everything once we've got some privacy."

I caught Jacquie's eye as she ushered Denise and Troy up the stairs. I'd half expected to see tears in her eyes or other signs she'd been crying. No, she was stone-faced and dry-eyed. Even in the face of potential heartbreak, my partner could keep her shit together. I admired that about her.

I was the last to enter the room. The three families clustered together, eying each other with a mixture of concern and suspicion. At least Jacquie understood the purpose of the get together. "I'm sorry to bring you all in like this, but the precinct wasn't the place to have the type of discussions we need to have," I began.

"Why are they here?" Mrs. Freeman asked, struggling to contain a squirming little boy. She had typical Asian features with a pale complexion and long, straight dark hair. The child in her lap had darker skin and a mess of curls.

"Their daughters were taken, too," I answered bluntly.

The looks of wariness melted instantly into ones of sympathy. Mrs. Ramirez reached over and squeezed Melissa Freeman's hand. Mr. Ramirez gave Jacquie an understanding look.

"You think it's the same person?" Denise said, still keeping her distance from the group.

"That is the theory we are working under. I know from some of our interviews that Neveah and Carly were friends. Did Gabby spend time with them, too?" I looked to Mrs. Freeman.

"Yes, she was friends with them. They went to different schools, but they all met here for afternoon sessions. They were all so excited about learning to use their gifts. It was all Gabby talked about." She wiped tears from her cheeks and held the child in her lap just a little tighter.

"What sort of skills were the girls developing?" I probed.

"They all thought they could do whatever they wanted. They didn't care if they were supposed to be one thing or another because of what we have ability wise," Mrs. Ramirez said with a small smile.

Her response wasn't surprising given kids' attitudes in general especially about not wanting to be defined by their families. As someone who grew up painfully aware of the family legacy I carried, I envied their ability to cast off those expectations and do whatever they wanted.

"Neveah was studying healing and medicine. She said she wanted to be a doctor when she grew up," Jacquie offered.

"Carly has always been more athletic, but the minute Neveah wanted to study healing, she insisted she did, too. I think she had a crush on one of the instructors."

"Gabby definitely did. She talked about him all the time," Mrs. Freeman added.

I was biased, but their teacher was quite something to look at. It was one of the reasons I was dating him. "I'll make a note to talk to J.T., then."

"No, not him. One of the older kids who helped out. Oh, what's his name ..." Mrs. Freeman sighed.

"Adrian," Troy interjected.

I turned to him. "Adrian Baptiste. Are you sure?"

He nodded. "I heard them talking about him sometimes. Stupid girl stuff about how cute he is and everything. It was definitely Adrian. She was all pissed he hadn't been around lately."

The more I learned about Adrian, the less I liked where it was going. He seemed like such a nice kid when I'd first met him. A little weird and gawky, but I hadn't been in great shape when we'd first crossed paths. I'd chalked his reaction up to the fact I'd come in bleeding and battered. *Was his unspoken curiosity more than just learning from his mother?*

"That information really helps, thank you Troy."

"He was always so nice to Carly. He even offered to tutor her for regular school," Mr. Ramirez protested.

"We're going to follow every avenue we have to bring the girls home. Can you think of any other people the girls might have come into contact with who knew they had magic? I'm assuming they knew enough to keep quiet about it, even if they wanted to explore other avenues."

"Gabby never mentioned anyone. And I monitor all of her computer and phone time," Mrs. Freeman answered.

"We would know if Carly was talking to anyone she wasn't supposed to, too. We checked her computer twice a week without warning so she wouldn't have time to delete things," Mrs. Ramirez added.

I locked eyes with Jacquie. "How was Neveah's computer usage monitored?"

"She was only on the computer to do homework. She knew better than to pull anything shady. Not with me around," Jacquie answered.

I needed to dig deeper into what the girls talked about when their parents and guardians weren't looking. Preteen girls loved to gossip and they shared their deepest thoughts with each other. It was entirely possible their innermost thoughts were hidden away in Direct Messages on Twitter or Insta-gram. "I'm going to need access to the girls' computers and phones," I said.

"Gabby had hers with her when she was taken. Can't you track it to find where she is?" Mrs. Freeman interjected.

I made a mental note to have Avery ping the

phone. "We're working on that. I want you to bring their devices here, to Avery."

"Why not the actual police?" Denise scoffed.

"Because Avery knows how to find magical signatures in tech better than anyone. We're trying to keep the existence of magic a secret still. We don't need a department IT guy stumbling through a group chat about harnessing unseen mystical energies," I answered more harshly than I'd intended.

After a brief moment of uncomfortable silence, she and Troy led the small group back down to the first floor. Leaving Jacquie and I standing opposite each other, a cluster of chairs separating us.

"Why does this kid keep popping up?" Jacquie mused.

"I don't know, but I think it's time to find out. I'm going to talk to Belladonna again. Maybe see if J.T. knows anything else about Adrian's interactions with the girls. It's not a coincidence that he knew all three of them and he goes missing right before they do," I said.

"But what motive would he have?"

I wish I knew.

SEVENTEEN

I didn't have to go far to find Belladonna. She was sequestered in the library, poring over a book with such intensity I was almost afraid to disturb her.

"Belladonna," I said loudly enough to catch her attention.

"Uh ... is there any news?" She didn't look up from the book.

"Some, but I also have a few more questions for you," I said and took the seat beside her.

She set the book down and faced me. She no longer looked like the kind, gentle woman I'd met months ago who healed me without question. She looked tired and beaten down. "What did you find?"

I sucked in a breath and said, "We found footage of him arriving to and leaving from South Station. It looked like he was alone, but he made a phone call to someone as he was leaving."

"You found his phone. You can see who he called, right?" A tiny glimmer of hope brightened her face.

"He used a different phone. Probably a cheap one he bought at a convenience store. He tossed his other phone in the trash. That's what led us to the station in the first place."

"Why would he do that?"

A few reasons came to mind, none of them good. *An illicit romance. Planning a kidnapping or three.* "Can I see your phone?"

"Mine? He didn't call me. I wouldn't have reported him missing if he'd called me."

"I just need to be sure. We're doing the same thing with your ex-husband's phone."

"You spoke with him?"

"I did. He filled me in on his family's type of magic. I'm not surprised a teenage boy who didn't know his father would be interested in learning about using magic to commune with the dead if that meant finding a connection to his father." About a year after my mother's death, I'd tried a séance to commune with her spirit. It had failed in spectacular fashion, maybe that was because I didn't have the right gifts.

A sour expression pulled her lips into a pout. "Let me guess, he told you they don't raise the dead. That it's disrespectful to the spirits of those who passed on."

"Pretty much. Is that not the case?"

She let out a bitter laugh. "He has a niece who advertises as a necromancer. Raising the dead so people can have one last conversation with their loved ones."

"So, she conducts séances?"

"No. She gives them a physical body. It's as if the dead are right there in the room with you. Maybe Adrian tried to reach out to her."

More death and darkness. Awesome. "I'll have Jacquie look into it."

"You're not working his case?" She said.

"I know you came to me, because I'm the Savior. However, we are working a serial kidnapping case with three missing girls who we know for certain didn't go willingly. One of them is Jacquie's niece, another is Carly Ramirez, remember?"

"Oh lord ... That's why they were at the police station yesterday. They must be terrified."

"They are, but they're hanging in there. All three were in training with Adrian—Carly Ramirez, Gabby Freeman, and Neveah DeWitt. It sounds like they had a bit of a crush on Adrian. Did you ever notice if he took an interest in any of them beyond training?"

"I don't like where this is going," she said, giving me side-eye.

"I was told he tutored Carly and that he babysat her when she was younger."

Her shoulders relaxed by a fraction of an inch. "Yes, he was helping her in science. It was a way to earn a little extra money since he wasn't old enough to work a normal job, yet."

"Where did they usually study? I'm assuming it was supervised." I replied.

"Here." She gestured to the room around us. "They kept the door open, but I wasn't always watching them."

"So you don't know what they talked about during that time? If he asked Carly about her family's magic?"

"What do you mean?"

"When I met Mrs. Ramirez, she was using scrying crystals to try and find Carly's location. I know I've been out of touch for a while, but that's not something you see a lot around here."

Belladonna gave a dismissive snort. "Not everyone in this community is as tolerant of old ways that didn't come from white people. If they did talk about it, I suspect it was to commiserate about that fact."

I wanted to tell her that we weren't like that anymore, but I'd be lying. Besides I wasn't going to get anywhere in finding any of these kids by feeding her a line of bullshit she could spot a mile off. *Who knew kidnappings would mean cultural immersion?* A knock on the library door cut me off from making any kind of comment. We both turned to see Jacquie standing in the doorway. Her face still had that stony, masked quality.

"What's wrong?" I got to my feet before she answered.

"Do you know someone named Natalia Baptiste?" She directed the question to Belladonna.

"She's my ex-husband's niece." Belladonna looked at me. "The one I told you about"

Jacquie turned to me. "The techs found messages between them on Adrian's computer. They were arranging to meet."

I pinched the bridge of my nose and exhaled slowly, fixing my gaze on Belladonna. "You said she is a necromancer. Do you know where she operates?"

"I don't. I broke ties with that side of the family a long time ago. I only know what she does since she sent me a flyer about her shop a few months ago, trying to drum up business."

I added finding Natalia to my list of to-dos right along with tracking down Lola Cox, rescuing three missing girls, and possibly beating the magical shit out of some Order lackeys.

Belladonna stood and reached a hand out to grab my wrist. "I know you think Adrian is involved in what happened to those girls, but you're wrong. Whatever he was doing with his cousin, I'm sure it had nothing to do with it."

I forced a tight-lipped smile and said nothing. Parents don't always know their children as well as they think. Then again, the same is true in reverse. I thought I'd known who my parents were and spent a decade blaming my father for something he didn't do. I had let rage build against a phantom that didn't exist. Jacquie and I retreated to the front driveway.

"She's wrong, you know," I said, fishing the car keys from my pocket. "It isn't a coincidence he went missing before them and that he had prior contact with all three of them."

"I agree with you, but we still don't have a motive."

"No, but we've got a lead we didn't have an hour ago." Time for us to make friends with a necromancer.

EIGHTEEN

A quick records search gave us the location of a new-age shop owned by one Natalia Baptiste nestled amongst the high-end boutiques on Newbury Street. How she managed to afford the space, I had no idea. A tiny bell above the door announced our presence, tinkling in the air with an echo a bell of its size shouldn't have. Even before I stepped foot inside, I could sense a cacophony of magical scents. Some were soothing like eucalyptus and rosemary, but mixed with other less pleasant ones like sulfur and rotting wood.

"Are you all right?" Jacquie prompted when I halted at the doorway.

"There are a lot of magical signatures in there. Fresh like their owners just left. Either she's been doing some seriously weird shit or she's got a steady stream of customers who all have magic—not all of them are good."

"Do you need to cleanse your palette?" She gestured to the charm hanging around my neck.

"Honestly, I think that would make it worse," I replied, my stomach doing a flip at the thought.

For one thing, it would just give whatever signatures were in the shop more of a hold on me, vying for my attention. Plus, I realized I didn't know what Adrian's magic smelled like—never having been around him when he used it—so I wouldn't be able to tell if he'd been through the shop recently. *Damn it.* I'd be kicking myself for that lapse in judgment for a long time.

I let out some of my own magic, feeling it slide over my skin like water, washing away some of the overwhelming scents wafting from within. I felt my muscles relax and let out a sigh. "Let's do this."

I expected the atmosphere to be stale with the stench of death—even if hidden by so much magic—but it wasn't. There was a little bit of spice to the air that reminded me of fall.

"Coming," an alto voice called from somewhere in the back.

I couldn't decide whether it was better to present myself as Ezri the detective or Ezri the witch. My magical credentials hadn't impressed her uncle. I was still debating the decision in my head when a tall

African-American woman strode out in designer jeans and a dark red tank top. She wore her hair pulled into a twist at the nape of her neck. I couldn't see much resemblance to Adrian or even his father in her.

"How can I help you?" She asked with a small, unassuming smile.

Jacquie stepped forward, badge in hand saving me from how to introduce myself. "I'm Detective DeWitt. This is my partner Detective Trenton. Are you Natalia Baptiste?"

"I am. What can I do for you?"

"We were hoping to ask you a few questions."

"Of course. What's this about, if you don't mind me asking?" Natalia leaned on a small counter cluttered with multi-colored crystals.

"Your cousin, Adrian Baptiste," I answered.

"Okay." She took a step away from us and I caught a hint of thyme fill the air.

Is she warding herself against me? "He went missing and we've got messages between the two of you discussing plans to meet up," I said bluntly.

"We did exchange some messages. I hadn't seen him since he was a little kid, probably about three or four years old. He somehow got my email address and reached out a few months ago."

"Did you ever meet up?" Jacquie probed.

"I told him he could come by the shop any time, but he never showed up. Believe me, if I knew something about where he'd gone, I'd tell you."

"Why do you think he reached out to you after all this time?" I had an idea of his motives. If he couldn't get his father to talk about their family's brand of magic, he'd find someone who would. Someone who practiced it openly.

"He was curious about our family's heritage," she said, eying both Jacquie and I warily.

"We know about your family's connection to the dead. You don't have to hide your magic," I replied.

I expected her to sigh in relief and drop whatever spell she was holding tight around herself. Instead, she tightened it, pouring more energy and power into it. I let the world around me fade just enough to catch the outline of her spell. Not so different from the one Jonathan had cast to make himself look normal. I reached a metaphysical hand out, found the edge of her magic and tugged. The air burst with a flurry of strawberry and thyme warring with one another for dominance. In the end my magic came out stronger and her spell vanished. A phone sat on the counter that I hadn't noticed. I tugged a loose latex glove from my pocket, using it to grab the phone before stopping her from hiding it again.

"Wait, don't," she protested as I turned it on.

It was a burner phone with no lock screen. I exerted just the tiniest bit of magic to get me around the fact latex and touch screens don't mix and scrolled through the call history. There were only a couple of calls, all from the same number. At least one of them matched the date and time of Adrian's mystery call from the bus terminal.

"He called you the day he disappeared. What aren't you telling us?" I slid the phone into an evidence bag and stowed it in my pocket.

"I'd also like to remind you, we can charge you with obstruction if you don't cooperate," Jacquie noted coolly.

Natalia wouldn't meet either of our gazes as she leaned back against the counter. "Okay, yes, he called me a couple times. I thought he was trying to make sure I was around so he could come by. I said he never showed. He didn't, that's the truth. But the last time he called me, he said he appreciated getting back in touch with me. He'd found someone else who could help him more with learning about our family's gifts."

"Did he happen to mention who that someone was or how he met them?" I prodded.

"No. He didn't. I'm not close with his mom's side of the family. I mean, sure I sent her a flyer when I first opened. I was just trying to get business, you know? And I don't really see my uncle very often. I didn't think anything was wrong when he just dropped off. I figured he was just off being a teenager. But you really think something bad happened to him?"

"We do," Jacquie said with a nod.

Natalia turned her attention to me. "You've got

strange magic." She gave a vague hand gesture toward my body. "I've never seen someone with so many auras floating around."

I blinked. "Sorry?"

"Everyone has an aura, whether they've got magic or not. Still people with power, theirs is different. It stands out and if you know how to look for it, you can spot other practitioners."

It made sense. In a way it was what I did when tracking magical signatures. Although I'd never seen any other magic around myself except my own. "Right. Their signature. But I've got just one."

Natalia shook her head. "You don't. You might only be able to sense your own, but there's dozens, all woven together. I've never met anyone with that much power."

My hand moved to the pentacle at my neck, but I said nothing. "I'm the Savior," I offered instead.

I watched her turn to blink in confusion. "The savior of what exactly?"

I bit back an annoyed sigh and answered, "Back during the Witch Trials, my ancestor's sister had a prophecy about one of the family line being The One to take on a rising darkness."

"That's a lot of responsibility for one person to carry," she noted, picking up on the capitalization in my tone.

"I'm used to it," I said with a shrug.

Natalia went quiet while regarding Jacquie and

I, squinting at my partner, no doubt trying to figure out how she was involved in all this magic craziness. "I'm sorry I hid the phone from you. I really am. I swear, if he reaches out again, I will let you know."

I passed her my card. "I'll hold you to that." Jacquie turned on her heel and left the shop. I was about to follow her when a thought occurred to me. "You serve a lot of magical people."

"That sounds like a statement rather than a question."

"Let's just say I have a knack for picking up on magical signatures. This place is crawling with dozens and not all of them good. You might want to be a little choosier with who you deal with. There are dangerous people out there."

She gave me a sad smile. "I know, Detective. Believe me, I know. I wish you all the best in finding Adrian. When you do, smack him for me for being such a thoughtless idiot to make everyone worry so much."

I didn't respond, but didn't hide my amusement either. We weren't exactly closer to finding Adrian or the girls, but I had to admit I was getting quite the magical education.

NINETEEN

"DeWitt, I thought I told you to go home and be with your family," Captain Beech barked when we arrived back at the precinct.

"Captain, as you pointed out, I had another missing person's case. There's no conflict in her working that one," I intervened.

The captain gave me a sidelong look before pointing from me to the conference room. "We've got guests."

Icy tendrils of dread crawled over my skin as I approached the room. I spotted a snatch of navy-blue windbreaker and my heart skipped a beat. She'd called in the feds after all. Swallowing the sizeable lump in my throat—that I swore tasted like Taggart's magic—I walked in. The team was smaller than last time. A woman with bleach blond hair pulled into a loose braid down her back stood at the head of the table. She looked up as the door swung shut behind me.

"You must be Detective Trenton," she said, rounding the table and offering her hand. "Agent Molly Cartwright."

"I'm guessing my reputation precedes me," I said uneasily.

"I knew Jamison Taggart and honestly, him being involved in that serial homicide case didn't surprise me. He always seemed a little off to me."

"So, how much has the Captain told you about the kidnappings?" The less I had to think about that bastard the better.

"She wanted you to fill us in, seeing as you're the lead detective."

Heat crept up the nape of my neck. "Well, so far we've had three abductions in less than forty-eight hours which is unusual. We've got a tech specialist analyzing available surveillance footage from the scenes."

"I'm assuming you've established victimology?"

Here's where things get dicey. "We believe so. All three girls come from mixed heritage families, are similar ages and all knew one another. It's possible their abductor was aware of their connection."

"And no one in their circles seems like a fitting suspect?"

"They were in an after-school program and one of the older kids there was a bit of a crush for the girls. Unfortunately, he went missing before the girls did."

Agent Cartwright turned to the board with all of the pertinent information about the girls' disappearances. "That certainly does read as suspicious."

"Except eye witnesses in two of the cases reported seeing a Caucasian woman with either brown or black hair approaching the girls right before they disappeared."

"How do you explain them just disappearing from the footage?" Agent Cartwright wondered aloud.

She had no idea that magic was real or that it was intertwined with this case. I didn't have any answers to give her that wouldn't expose our secret. "No idea," I lied.

She rubbed her chin and looked back at me with a sympathetic expression in her eyes. "I don't blame you for being leery of working with us after what happened last time. I want to assure you that I'm not like him. But I also know words don't mean as much as actions. If you'll let me, I'd like to prove to you that I can be an ally."

"I appreciate that. I am working a possible lead on a person of interest, but I don't want to get your hopes up. Let me vet the information I've gotten first. I promise I'll bring you up to speed if it turns out to be something," I said.

"Bit of a lone wolf, aren't you?" She smirked.

"Something like that." I retreated to my desk, intent on finding out what I could about Lola Cox. I'd pegged her as our kidnapper on the word of a shady bartender, but I needed more if I was going to make a credible arrest under the FBI's watchful gaze. Even if Agent Cartwright claimed to be on my side, she could still tank this if I wasn't careful.

I typed in Lola's name, praying it wasn't an alias. An electronic file popped up with a list of various offenses ranging from possession of illegal drugs to conspiracy to commit robbery. Kayla said she had fallen in with a rough crowd. *Didn't think it was quite that rough.* Lola's mug shot was probably close to a decade old. She looked to be in her early twenties and had mousy brown hair that hung limply around her face like a curtain. I scrolled down to the section on identifying marks. There was an entry from three years ago with a photo of her hand and a very distinctive triple spiral and scythe.

"That looks like a nasty brand," Agent Cartwright said from behind me, making me jump.

"Yeah. Some people are into weird shit," I said.

"Guessing that's your person of interest?" She bent to study the file over my shoulder. "Seems a stretch to go from knocking over liquor stores to snatching kids."

"Like I said, I'm not even sure it's anything useful. I'll let you know if I'm even able to track her down. For all we know, she's not even in town anymore."

"Keep me in the loop," she said before heading off to intercept Captain Beech at the coffee machine.

Waiting until Jonathan actually called me, there was little I could do. I needed to get back home and study my mother's books. See if they held the answers like Theodora suggested. As the sun began its descent into evening, a sense of foreboding settled over me. Carly had less than twenty-four hours left if we had any hope of a positive outcome.

JUNE 21, 2017

TWENTY

An empty tinfoil wrapper from a burrito sat on the table as I poured over the books detailing the Authority's history. I wasn't sure what I was looking for exactly. As I turned yet another carefully preserved page, my phone buzzed with an alert. I glanced at it only to realize it was after midnight. The tiny notification on the screen cheerily reminded me that today was the Solstice.

The one day in the whole year where light magic was at its height. When casting spells and pouring out one's intent was made all that much easier. I sighed at the realization that maybe this was a sign that things were looking up. That maybe we had a real shot at bringing Adrian, Carly, Neveah, and Gabby home safe after all.

Setting my phone aside, I went back to the books. Instead of just randomly flipping through and hoping to come across something useful, I placed my palms down on the pages, tapping into the renewed energies around me. If they'd jumped to my will two days ago, the unseen force around me practically cascaded over me in an effort to aid my spell.

"Show me ways to confine someone," I murmured.

The ripest strawberries burst around me and the pages went warm beneath the pads of my fingers. I didn't dare open my eyes until the warmth faded and my magic receded. I peered down at the pages beneath my fingers to find an entry on a binding circle. The entry complete with illustration and careful notes on what was best to use to ensure dark magics couldn't cross it and fight back.

"Okay, that's pretty damn cool," I said to my empty apartment.

It seemed something as simple as a ring of salt could confine most people with magic, but the stronger they were, the more likely they'd be able to cross the barrier. Given what I'd seen on tape of Lola's abilities, salt wasn't going to do anything to keep her confined. I spotted a small scribble at the bottom of the page in different handwriting. Writing I could swear wasn't there a moment ago. It simply read: mortal iron.

What the hell is mortal iron?

No one was around to answer my question, obviously. So, I set my hands back on the pages, called up more power and whispered, "What is mortal iron?"

The pages warmed to my touch again and when I opened my eyes, the pages beneath my palms were blank. I started to lift my hands when something sharp impaled the meat of my palms, drawing blood. It dribbled onto the pages, spelling out 'mortal iron' in the same handwriting as the other page.

"Awesome," I sighed. If I wanted to keep Lola properly contained, I was going to need to bleed and a lot. I may be the savior, but I'm not indestructible. Far from it in fact.

Just as I contemplated going the salt route and praying the signal boost of the Solstice would be enough to keep her from taking off, my phone skittered across the table with an incoming text message from an unknown number.

'Our mutual friend is here. Don't make me regret this, Savior.'

Vague much? I had to assume it was Jonathan. At least he wasn't a completely heartless jackass. I took the stairs down to the first floor at a rapid pace—momentarily wishing I actually could teleport—before I pulled away from my building in the direction of Notre Dame.

THE BOUNCER SAW me walking up the street and put himself in the path of the door.

"Relax, your boss gave me a personal invite this time," I said.

"You won't mind if I check with him?" He said in a gruff tone.

I had no idea if he was stalling, but I needed as few people pissed off at me as possible so I said, "Go ahead."

He pulled a walkie talkie from his belt, pressed the 'Talk' button and said, "Boss, that lady detective's here."

I didn't appreciate the dig at my gender, but I stayed silent. "Let her in," Jonathan replied.

Mr. Bouncer reattached the radio to his belt and shoved the door open for me. I caught whispers going down the line of people waiting to get in. More than half stepped out of line, clearly not wanting to be anywhere near the police—smart people.

The bass thumped from the dance floor just like it had the night before. I scanned the crowd, taking a breath, trying to find Lola's magic. Nothing yet. Although that didn't mean Jonathan was lying to me. I sauntered up to the bar and slid onto one of the few barstools. I caught his eye and he set a tiny umbrella in a glass, passing it to a waitress before moving down my way.

"This makes us square, right?" He said above the throb of the music.

"Depends on if she's actually here," I answered.

He pointed to a table near the DJ setup. "She's right there. Now, do me a favor and don't ruin my night by messing up my establishment."

"Believe me, it's not my intention." Somehow, I doubted Lola was the type to come quietly, especially when she was surrounded by a ton of other people with magic who probably didn't like me.

I got within two feet of their table before a literal fireball whizzed past my head. The heat it generated was enough to make my hair stand on end. People screamed and the dance floor became a stampede of people making for the exit.

"Was that a *fireball?*" A voice called from behind me.

I turned to see Agent Cartwright standing there gawking at me. *Shit, what's she doing here?* "Get down!" I yelled, tackling her to the floor and dragging her behind the protection of an upended table as another ball of white-hot flame whizzed by.

"How is he doing that?" She rasped in awe.

I glanced around the edge of the table to find Lola was still visible, which was perplexing. I expected her to pull a literal disappearing act while her buddies laid down cover. A third fireball was in the works and this time I wasn't going to let him get that far. I held out a hand, pouring out will into the air around me, letting it be an extension of my body. *Make it cold as ice.* The air around his hands turned smoky with cool vapors and his fire died down. He yelped as his hands turned paler and paler with frostbite.

"Don't be a pussy, Freddy," Lola spat at the temporarily incapacitated pyro.

"Did you ... what the hell is going on?" Agent Cartwright demanded.

"Not now," I snapped. I needed a way to stop this before we had to explain things to the fire department. I took a deep breath, called my magic up like a shield and darted to the bar. "Salt. Give me salt, now," I yelled at Jonathan.

"Why in the hell?" he started, but shook his head and passed me a container. "I'm charging the city for this damage."

"You do you, buddy," I muttered and retreated to the table where Agent Cartwright huddled, weapon in hand. "That's not going to help here," I noted and held out the bucket of salt.

"What's that for?"

"Just take a handful and do exactly as I say. I need you to cover me and flank them. Lay down a circle of this around them."

"What's that going to do?"

"Probably piss them off, but hopefully give me a chance to do what I came here to do. Now, move."

I charged forward, dropping the shield to give them a moving target so hopefully they wouldn't notice the FBI agent binding them with salt. I wasn't ready to bleed for this, not yet.

"I just want to talk to you, Lola. That's all," I said.

"What makes you think I'm interested in talking?" She shot back.

Her hot-handed pal fell back as I sprinkled salt by Lola's feet. "You're still here, for one thing. I know what you're capable of. The fact you didn't turn and run says you're interested in what I've got to say."

In my periphery, I spotted Agent Cartwright sprinkling her handful of salt on the floor around Lola. The young man who'd been standing by Lola's other side—he didn't look old enough to be in here legally—started to distance himself from the situation. Not a bad move until he bumped into my impromptu backup.

To her credit, Agent Cartwright wrapped her forearm around his windpipe, incapacitating him in seconds. Hot-Hands was shaking off the last vestiges of frostbite as I tried to figure out a way to get the rest of the circle closed. Instead of lobbing another fireball at me, he lunged and was halted midair by something I couldn't see. The air smelled strongly of lemons and I turned just enough to see Jonathan holding his hand out over the bar.

"Get the fuck out of my bar you little shit," he snapped and flung the wannabe pyro toward the door. The guy scrambled to his feet and darted out the front. "You can get out, too," he said, hooking a thumb in my direction.

"Thanks, but we're sticking around. Police business," I said and turned back to Lola. Agent Cartwright had managed to finish the circle. I honestly had no idea if this would even work.

From my left, Agent Cartwright coughed dramatically. I kept an eye on Lola who remained mute in the center of our makeshift binding circle as I stepped over to the agent.

"I'd really like to know what the *hell* is going on," she hissed.

Do I lie? She's already seen magic first hand. Besides it wasn't like non-magical people weren't brought in on the secret. Jacquie was a prime example. *Screw it, if being the Savior doesn't give me a little flexibility, then what's the point?* "Magic is real. I'm descended from a long line of witches and I basically averted the apocalypse three months ago."

I expected her to call me a liar or tell me I needed a psych eval. Instead, she bent double, hands pressed to her knees and laughed. Her whole body shook and when she finally straightened, her eyes shone with tears.

"I'm sorry, the apocalypse? Really?"

I blinked. "Of everything I just said, *that's* what you're having trouble with?"

"I mean what does that even look like?"

"Uh, raising long-dead evil druids to do God knows what," I said matter-of-factly.

She wiped the tears from her eyes and gathered her composure. "So, you can just make fireballs and throw people around like rag dolls?"

"Personally, I'm not a big fan of the destruction of property or assault, but technically, yeah."

"And you what ... use these skills to solve cases?"

"Yup." I glanced at Lola who looked exceedingly bored by the whole conversation. "Look, I'll answer your questions later, but right now, we've got an interrogation to conduct."

"Not in my damn bar, you don't," Jonathan protested. When I turned to look at him, I took half a step back. He'd dropped the spell giving him a normal appearance to reveal a large hump over his left shoulder. His biceps—which had already been impressive—tripled in size and thickness. He'd even grown half a foot. His face remained handsome as ever with those dark eyes and sharp jawline. Guilt tied a knot in my stomach at the thought of him as handsome. *I have a very attractive boyfriend.*

"Come on, Johnny," I said, trying to sound unfazed by his transformation.

"I'm not stupid enough to hit a cop, but you are really trying my patience, Savior."

"Please, let me just do this here and we'll be square. You have my word."

"You've yanked me around before, Detective."

I pressed a hand to my heart. "I swear. We'll be good and I won't darken your bar again."

"You don't really think I'm going to help you." Lola joined the conversation. She kicked her toe against the barrier of salt. It scuffed the floor, clearly not doing anything useful. "Some Savior you are."

I could have smacked myself. Of course, just a circle of salt wasn't going to do anything on its own. All magic needs intent, direction and I'd had someone who had no magic to speak of lay it down. My body was in motion before my brain had time to catch up. Strawberries overtook Jonathan's lemon scent and a tiny knife used to slice lemons and limes flew out from behind the bar, landing in my outstretched hand.

"What are you doing?" Agent Cartwright called as I slid the blade across my palm.

I winced in pain as blood welled up along the cut, pooling in my cupped hand. I wasn't sure it was going to work. Not until I bent down, pressed my bloody hand to the line of salt and put out my intent into the world. *Bind her.*

The circle snapped closed around Lola's feet and a visible barrier of shimmery light shot up to the ceiling. Lola pressed a finger to it and gave an irritated yelp as it zapped her.

"Oh, fuck. Ow," I cursed, as the realization of pressing salt into an open wound caught up to my senses.

Agent Cartwright darted behind the bar, returning with a cloth and some water. Wordlessly, she began tending to my hand. I sucked in a steadying breath and waited for the pain to subside.

"Now that you're not going anywhere, let's chat, Ms. Cox," I said.

"Go to hell."

"Where are the girls?" I stepped closer.

"What girls?" She replied, feigning an innocent look.

"Carly Ramirez. Neveah DeWitt. Gabby Freeman. I know you took them. What I don't know is why. And if anything happens to them, and I mean anything, you'll be charged as a co-conspirator. Isn't that right Agent Cartwright?" I glanced to the blond standing beside me.

"Indeed. And people who commit crimes against children are not welcomed in any prison with open arms."

Lola held up her hand to Agent Cartwright. "Prison doesn't scare me FBI lady. You don't know what this means, but she does. You can lock me up, but you can't stop what's coming. I won't be alone."

"Newsflash, the last person with that mark who ended up behind bars has by his own account been cut off. I'm pretty sure he's a hell of a lot more important than you," I quipped.

Lola let out a howl of anger and her right hand disappeared. The scent of brackish water permeated the barrier. She gave out a loud grunt as she pressed against the barrier. At least I assumed that's what she'd done because when she pulled back, her hand returned with burn marks.

"Are the Order really worth all this pain? I swear, I just want to bring these girls home safe to their families. I don't care about your past. Hell, I'd say it's pretty damn clever using a Whisperer to rob banks."

Agent Cartwright mouthed 'Whisperer,' but I ignored her. Lola cradled her injured hand to her chest and eyed us both. She didn't seem too bothered by the hulking form of the bartender.

"You really don't know what makes them so special do you?" Lola scoffed, narrowing her gaze at me.

"Enlighten me."

"Seriously, you're what's standing between us and success? Your side must be kicking itself, wondering how it ended up with such an idiot as their savior," she spat.

Maybe this wasn't going to work after all. I waved a hand at the barrier and it blinked out of existence. I looked to Agent Cartwright. "Can I borrow your cuffs?"

"What exactly are we charging her with?" She handed the cuffs over anyway.

"Resisting arrest. Plus, I've got a witness. If she's positively identified then we've got her for kidnapping," I answered. I didn't need Lola to know she'd just given herself away.

I scuffed the circle of salt just to be sure before I grabbed Lola's wrists, locking them in place with the handcuffs. For good measure I scooped up some of the bloody salt and rubbed them onto the metal, willing them to keep her confined again. I looked around at the bar. The tables were scattered and I could see a few char marks, but it didn't seem to be irreparable damage. To Jonathan I said, "I'll see what I can do to get the Authority to cover this for you."

Lemons popped in the air as he wrapped himself in his guise, returning his form to the bartender with the wicked smile. "I'll hold you to that, Detective. Now, for the last time ... Get out of my bar!"

TWENTY-ONE

I wasn't going to wake Troy in the middle of the night to do an ID. Lola could sit in holding for a few hours. I led her to the cell and released her wrists from the metal bracelets, making sure to get a little of the salt on the bars.

"You even think of walking through walls and I swear to God I will hunt you down. You think you don't like me now? You'll really hate me then. Understand?"

She rolled her eyes. "So scary." She plunked herself onto one of the empty benches in holding and waved her hands around. "I'm not going anywhere."

I found Agent Cartwright in the conference room just staring at the whiteboard. I slid her cuffs back to her along the table. "I'm guessing you've got questions."

"Just a few. But I'm guessing here's not the best

place." She glanced at her phone. "Care for an early breakfast?"

"Why not."

Not many places were open this early and we ended up driving around until we found a little diner out in the suburbs. A beleaguered waiter poured us coffee and left us alone to browse the menus.

"Is it safe to talk here?" Agent Cartwright asked.

"Yeah. I'm pretty sure we're fine, Agent Cartwright."

"Please, call me Molly." She poured a generous stream of sugar into her coffee, swirling her spoon in quick circles.

"Sure. So, what do you want to know? Before you go too far, you should know I was out of touch with things for a while. It's complicated and I'd rather not get into it right now."

"So, where does it come from? Magic." She whispered the last word as if saying it too loudly would make the world end or something.

"It's a natural force that exists around us and in those of us who know how to use it. It's in our blood."

"So, it's genetic," she said, leaning forward, hands grasping her coffee mug tight.

"I guess. Magic passes through the maternal line. Don't ask me why. It's just the way it is."

"I'm guessing there's good magic and bad magic."

I shook my head. "No. Magic doesn't take sides. It's about how you choose to use it. You can save lives. Hell you could probably find a way to cure cancer if you put enough intent out into the world. Or you know, you can kill people."

"The bartender and Ms. Cox, they both called you the savior. I'm guessing that's not a common thing."

"No. My ancestor's sister made a prophecy back during the Witch Trials that I'd come along to stop the darkness. That darkness happens to be called the Order of Samael. The mark on Lola's hand is their brand. You'd have found it on Jamison Taggart's wrist, too."

"So, they're what ... a secret society?"

"Something like that. From my experience, they're out to hurt people for the sake of doing it. Like I said, three months ago they tried to resurrect some seriously nasty druids. Taggart was at the helm of that little operation. If I hadn't managed to stop them, I don't know what would have happened. We averted that crisis."

"When was this exactly?"

"The Equinox. During the meteor shower and the eclipse."

"Huh. That all kind of makes sense now. So, how does magic work exactly? Can you fly?" Her cheeks flushed with color and she bowed her head. "I don't know why I asked that."

"No, I can't fly. Magic has limits and conse-quences. You strain yourself too much and you get things like nose bleeds or massive migraines. Sometimes your magic can turn against you and you end up being able to walk through walls and turn invisible like Lola. That's what Whisperers are. Their magic has turned them into something else."

"Fascinating. What about the bartender? He wasn't exactly what I'd call normal."

"Frankly, I've never met anyone like him before. Not that I know every magical person in the city. Far from it. Still I don't know if that's just a legit medical condition he's hiding or if his magic went haywire on him."

She gulped down coffee, flagging down the waiter for a refill. He appeared at the table looking tired and bored, but offered up a fresh pot of coffee and dutifully vanished when we didn't need him anymore. He didn't even seem annoyed that we weren't ordering food.

"Anyway, the way magic works is you need to be able to harness the energy from within yourself and the world around you, then pour out your intent. Like at the bar, I willed the circle to bind Lola and it did."

"I'm not totally up on my moon phases and such, but isn't the Summer Solstice coming up?"

"It's today actually."

"That's important, I'm guessing.'

I leaned back and regarded the agent across the booth from me. She was picking up quick. A part of me—the part that had taught me to distrust easily—wanted to question her curiosity and her ready acceptance of such a bombshell. Although, she didn't exude any hint of magic. I didn't see what probing for basic information would get her.

"Yes. The balance of power shifts with the seasons. Spring and Autumn things are pretty even. Summer gives the good guys an advantage and—"

"Winter gives the bad guys a leg up," she interrupted.

"Exactly." I sipped from my own mug. The cut on my hand ached. It gave me an excuse to pay my woefully neglected boyfriend a visit. Not that I really needed one.

"So, you've been using magic for this case?" Molly whispered.

"Not as much as you'd think. People have different gifts and for me, I can pick up on magical signatures if they've been used recently. I know what the kidnapper's magic smells like. When Lola turned her hand invisible, it gave off the same scent. You'll probably find she was wearing a wig or something in the video footage, but it's her."

"Well, let's hope we can convince her to grow a conscience before our window closes on the first victim."

"You should probably know my partner is working a separate missing person's case. Another kid from the community."

"Community?"

"The girls who were taken all come from magical families. So does the boy who Jacquie's looking for. He knew all three and spent time alone with at least one of them."

"Right. You mentioned that before. So, if you had to speculate about motive for taking these particular girls, what would it be?"

I scrubbed at my face with my uninjured hand. "I feel it has to do with their heritage. The Authority may look diverse on the outside, but there are cultural differences at play. Ones that get white-washed and I think maybe someone's taking advantage of that."

"What is this authority?" By the way she said it, I could tell she wasn't treating it like a proper noun.

"It's the good guy governing body. It was founded after the Witch Trials to try keeping order among our citizens and magic hidden from the wider world. Thirteen people sit on the Council. It's largely been hereditary if what I learned as a kid is accurate."

"Fascinating. Your partner knows about all of this?"

"Yeah. She knew who and what I was before we'd even met. Made for a bit of awkwardness when I found out, but she's been a good friend and an ally."

Molly set her mug aside as the late hour and the deluge of information caught up to her. Her skin sagged a little around her mouth and eyes. Her eyelids drooped slightly too. "I hope you know I want to be an ally."

I nodded. "I think you do." I glanced down at my hand. "Can you do some digging into Lola and see if you can find anything we can use to get her to flip on the Order?"

"I'll see what I can find. Where are you going?"

"I need to get this looked at."

TWENTY-TWO

At least I wasn't in as dire of a condition as when J.T. and I had first saw each other after a decade apart. I'd been recovering from being nearly stabbed to death. He answered the door looking more awake than I had expected.

"What's wrong?" He asked.

"Can't a girl just drop by to see her boyfriend?" I asked and held up my hand. "Also, I may have sliced my hand with a fruit knife."

"You don't own a fruit knife," he said and ushered me inside.

"Work-related injury," I added with a smile and kissed him on the cheek.

He pressed his palm to the small of my back and kissed my lips, holding me close for a long time. When he finally pulled away, he asked, "Do I want to know?"

"Hunting down a rogue Whisperer at a bar. I needed to keep her in one spot and apparently the best way to do that is with blood."

He peered at my hand and flicked a tiny grain of salt out of the wound. "Did you face plant in a bag of salt while you were at it?"

"It was more I tried the salt first and it didn't work. Hurt like hell, too."

He gave me another hug. "We both know you're capable of dealing with this on your own. But I appreciate you coming over," he said.

"I felt bad about the fact we haven't been spending a lot of time together lately," I admitted.

He led me to the tiny living room of his apartment and pointed to the couch. I sat dutifully and waited for him to return with a first aid kit. He pulled out a single piece of gauze and some medical tape. He sandwiched my palm between his hands and the honey scent of his magic washed over everything, forcing tension out of my neck and shoulders. He wrapped the gauze around my hand. "Keep that on for a few hours. Should be good as new after that."

I flexed my hand, watching the gauze strain against the tape. "Thanks."

"How's the case going? I know you can't give me specifics, but do you think there's a chance you'll find them in time?"

"There's a chance," I replied.

"Good," he sighed and settled next to me, arm draped around my shoulders.

I leaned into him and closed my eyes, taking in the lingering scent of his magic. It was comforting, lulling me into a light doze. Only his body shifting beneath mine roused me.

"How long was I out?" I mumbled, wiping sleep from my eyes.

"Not long," he answered.

I caught the hint of sunrise beyond his window. It had still been dark when I'd arrived. "As much as I don't want to, I probably should go and check in with Molly."

J.T. arched a brow. "Who is Molly?"

"FBI Agent I'm working with since Jacquie's off the case. She's looking into a person of interest."

I started for the door. "Did the girls ever talk about their family magic with you?"

"A little. They all said they were interested in learning about healing, but I'm pretty sure it was so they could hang out with the older kids. I think Carly mentioned once that her mom had told her stories about her ancestors being able to see the future. Why?"

I filed that away. "Just trying to figure out why these girls were taken. I'll let you know when we've got news. And we are doing a raincheck on dinner. Maybe a weekend away."

He pulled me in for a kiss, longer and deeper

than the last one. I didn't fight him. I pressed against him, letting his firm arms wrap around me in a tight embrace. Reminding me that I was loved and wanted, no matter the history between us. "I'll hold you to that," he said when we broke apart.

ON MY WAY back to the station, I called Jacquie and told her to have Denise and Troy come by the station. The sooner we had him identify Lola, the sooner we could get her into an interrogation room. I only hoped Molly had something we could use.

"She can't see me, right?" Troy asked as we stood in front of a window looking into a line up room.

"No. None of them can. They can't hear you either," I replied.

Molly stood next to Denise. A man in a rumpled suit and tie stood in the far corner. Lola had used her one phone call to bring in a shabby looking attorney. Not the one I'd seen going to bat for Taggart. It made sense if I'd pegged things correctly and Lola was low on the food chain of the Order.

"Take your time. There's no rush," Molly told Troy.

I focused on Lola—holding the number 4 card—and sent up a silent prayer that Troy would be able to identify her even if her hair color was different.

We had enough evidence to tie her to all three abductions.

"It's number four," Troy said with far more confidence than I'd expected.

"You're sure, honey?" Denise asked, eying the attorney on the other side of the room.

'Yes. That's her," he repeated.

Denise whirled on Molly, jabbing her finger at the window. "What are you waiting for? Make that bitch tell you where my baby girl is!"

"I'm sure we can come to some sort of agreement," the attorney offered in a flat tone. Lola clearly meant very little to him.

"Mrs. DeWitt, why don't you take Troy home and let us do our job," I said, pointing to the exit.

I rapped my knuckles on the glass four times and the officer inside ushered the six women out, separating Lola from the rest just outside of view. I stepped up to Molly and whispered, "Please tell me you have something we can use."

"I might have found something. Do you trust me?"

I opened my mouth to say 'yes.' Truthfully though we'd known each other less than twenty-four hours. I didn't have enough information on her to really give her that answer. "Enough to get us this far," I replied.

"I'll take it. Come on, we've got a kidnapper to interrogate."

I was used to Jacquie's interrogation style—direct, hard-hitting. I had no idea what Molly was going to do and not being able to anticipate her moves left me at a disadvantage. I would have felt better if she'd given me a hint of what she'd found to loosen Lola's lips. Trusting other people was a work in progress for me, I reminded myself. I trailed Molly to one of the interrogation rooms where Lola sat beside her attorney. He opened his mouth to speak when Lola cut him off.

"I'm not telling you anything. You've got one lousy witness and that's not enough to stand up in court," she said, leaning back in her chair like she'd won.

Molly arched a pale eyebrow at her, sat in one of the metal chairs on the other side of the table before quietly sliding a photo across the table. I tried not to crane my neck too hard to see what the photo contained. From my upside-down view it looked to be a young boy. By the way Lola's shoulders tensed and the color drained from her face, she recognized him.

"When's the last time you saw your little brother?" Molly's tone was calm, non-accusatory like she actually cared about the answer.

Lola's lips moved like she wanted to form words, but couldn't decide on what to say. The awkward silence was enough to rouse her attorney. "Look, what are you offering my client if she cooperates?"

"That depends on how helpful she is. After all, counselor, we've got three missing girls," Molly answered, never taking her eyes off the woman across from her "Come on, I really want to know about the last time you saw your brother."

Lola's composure slipped further as she studied the photo, her fingers twitching as she fought the urge to pull the image closer. *Damn, she's good.* Finally, Lola looked at Molly and said, "Three years ago. When they took him away from me. And you can't promise you'll get him back. No one's that powerful." Her gaze flicked to my face as she spoke her last words.

"The people you're working for, I'm betting they promised you that they'd reunite you if you did them a few favors, right?" I said, jumping into the interrogation. I had to be careful with what I said. I assumed her lawyer was in the know, but I didn't need some shitty defense attorney raving about magic if he wasn't aware of his client's supernatural skillset.

"You got nothing I want," Lola scoffed.

"Supervised visits to start with. Keeping you on the straight and narrow, maybe you get to see your baby brother without someone else in the room," I said before I could stop myself.

I caught the annoyed look on Molly's face out of the corner of my eye. She could be mad at me. I didn't care. I'd offer Lola the moon if it meant bringing the girls home safe. "What do you say? Come on, you know these girls have brothers and sisters, too. If someone took your brother, wouldn't you do everything in your power to get him back?"

"Look, I don't know where they are. It was above my paygrade. Besides, even if you do find them what makes you think they're ever going to be okay again?"

Her lawyer's eyes bugged out and he sat up straighter. Whatever he did or didn't know, he was paying attention to his client's words now. "I need a moment to confer with my client. Unless you're offering immunity from charges, we're not interested in talking further."

Molly and I slid our chairs back in unison and left the tiny room, stepping into silence beyond the glass partition. "That was good finding info on the brother," I commented.

"It wasn't hard to find. Just needed to look beyond her criminal history. But what you promised her in there, you have to know we can't do that. She's probably never going to be allowed near children ever again."

"Look, I'm not saying we should give her immunity, but the people she's working with are known to screw with people. Can't we give her a shot at redeeming herself even possibly a little bit?"

"And who exactly are the people she's working for?" Molly lowered her voice, giving a conspiratorial glance around us.

"I told you about the Order of Samael," I noted.

"You're positive they are the ones behind this?"

Gesturing to the two people speaking with their heads bent low in the interrogation room, I said, "You saw the brand on her hand. She's one of them. From what I've seen from the Order in the past, they don't generally like it when their people operate outside the lines. They like chaos and shit, but controlled chaos."

"We still don't know what they want with the girls."

Before I could comment, Lola's attorney waved his hand, knowing we could still see them even if we weren't privy to their conversation. I took the lead this time, sitting down across from Lola and making steady eye contact. "You going to try being a decent human being and avoid having us add worse charges than kidnapping to the list of things we can charge you with?"

"I want to talk to him. Before I tell you anything else, I want to talk to my brother in person. You do that for me, no tricks and I'll tell you what I know."

I bit back a growl of frustration. She was fucking with us, knowing our window for a marginally good outcome was closing fast. "We can work on that, but we need a show of good faith on your end, Lola. If you won't tell us where they are, can you at least tell us why them?"

She let out a laugh. "You don't know?"

I shook my head. I knew it was a risk to let her know how much I was off balance on this whole case. Still I also knew giving her that sense of having one up on me might make her more compliant. "Why don't you fill me in?"

"You're in for a world of pain when you figure out what's going on, Detective. You thought you stopped bad shit from going down before; you can't imagine what's coming for you."

I really wish the Order of Samael would stop underestimating me. "You say things like that and it makes me less inclined to get your brother down here." I glanced to Molly. "What about you Agent Cartwright? Maybe she's just bluffing and she doesn't know anything after all."

"Maybe you're right. If she really knew something useful and wanted to stay out of jail, she'd be spilling what she knows."

A sharp knock on the door cut off any further conversation. The door opened and Captain Beech appeared, giving Molly and I a sharp one-fingered summons. I pushed back from the table and gathered the photo of Lola's brother. She couldn't resist the reflex to grab for it anyway.

Wordlessly, I followed the captain out of the room while dreading whatever development she was about to lay on us. The three of us made it back to her office in silence.

"They found Carly Ramirez."

TWENTY-THREE

I didn't dare speak, too wrapped up in the gravity of the captain's words. *They found Carly Ramirez*. There were no qualifiers of where, when, or how. My brain began a downward spiral into all the terrible possibilities.

"Where? When?" Molly asked the questions I couldn't make my mouth form.

"About twenty minutes ago. She was spotted wandering on the Common. Dispatch received ten different calls reporting they saw her."

"So, she's alive," I breathed, relief cascading over me until the look of apprehension on the captain's face turned that wave into an icy chill.

"She's alive, but she's confused. She's being taken to Boston Medical for evaluation. I want you both to be there."

"We're on our way," I said, halfway out the door before Molly could get a word in edgewise.

"Hold on a minute. What about our suspect in interrogation?" Molly called as I headed for the parking lot.

I glanced over my shoulder. "We charge her with kidnapping and hold her while we go see what the hell these bastards did to a ten-year-old girl."

"It's not showing a lot of good will, reneging on the deal you offered her," Molly noted, falling into step beside me.

She had a point. I bit my bottom lip, suppressing a groan as I spun around and made a beeline for my desk. My fingers flew over the keys as I pulled up Lola's file and found the name of her brother's social worker. I copied it into my phone and gave Molly a nod.

"I'll reach out on the way over."

LOLA'S BROTHER'S social worker wasn't thrilled with the idea of a family reunion, but understood it was to help save lives. She promised to speak to Lola's brother and see if he was willing to see his sister. I shoved my hands into the pockets of my pants as we rode the elevator to the third floor.

"How many child victims have you dealt with?" Molly asked suddenly.

I swallowed. "None, but I'm not stupid. I'm not going to drill her if that's what you're worried about."

"I know we haven't known each other long, but from what I've observed, rushing in is kind of your go-to move. I just don't want you to have that be what throws a roadblock into this case."

Anger bubbled in my chest, making it hard to breathe. I clamped down on my tongue to keep myself from saying something antagonistic. I needed all the allies I could get and telling her she was wrong—when she was probably more accurate than I wanted to admit—wouldn't do anyone any good. Molly stared at me in silence as I composed myself. After a few tense moments I gave her a nod. "You're right. I'm good."

She gestured for me to take the lead and I approached the hospital room with a uniformed officer posted outside. Smart move. I held up my badge and the officer inspected it before giving us a nod to enter. I braced myself for what was to come only to find Carly lying in the hospital bed, one parent on either side of her. She looked tired and the skin around her mouth was dry, but otherwise she appeared unharmed—on the outside at least.

I approached with slow steps, letting her see my badge so she hopefully understood I was there to help her. "Hi Carly, I'm Detective Trenton. This is Special Agent Cartwright. How are you feeling?"

Carly blinked up at me with no recognition in

her face. She turned her head first to look at her father and then her mother. "I don't understand why I'm here."

"What did they do to her?" Mrs. Ramirez wept, grasping her daughter's right hand in a vise grip.

I leaned on the edge of the bed. "Carly, can you tell me the last thing you remember?"

She pressed her lips together in thought and I waited until she spoke again. "I was getting groceries. The T was really crowded. Then ... I was on the Common. But I don't remember walking there. How did I get there? What's going on?" Her voice pitched into a whine by the end of the question.

"That's what we're going to find out," I said in a soft tone.

Carly sunk back against the pillows and pressed her face into her mother's shoulder. Mr. Ramirez gave her other hand a squeeze before relinquishing his grip and gesturing for Molly and I to join him in the hallway.

"How can she not remember where she's been?" He asked in a whisper.

"It's possible whoever took her gave her something to disrupt her short-term memory," Molly said.

Mr. Ramirez gave me a look that clearly asked if magic was involved. "Let's wait to see what the doctors say about her condition."

On cue, a tall doctor approached with clipboard

in hand. "Mr. Ramirez?" He didn't acknowledge Molly or I.

"Yes?"

"Can I speak with you and your wife in private for a moment?"

Mr. Ramirez cast me a concerned look. "What about the police? If it is about Carly, they need to know whatever it is you found."

The doctor's gaze skated over me and I met his look with a determined one of my own. "Yes, of course. Sorry officers."

"Detective," I said on autopilot.

"Special Agent," Molly added in the same defensive tone.

At least I wasn't alone in clinging to the rank I'd earned. Color warmed his cheeks for a split second before he gestured toward Carly's hospital room. Mr. Ramirez stepped inside, returning a few seconds later with his wife. She dabbed at fresh tears on her cheeks.

"What did they do to our baby girl?" She asked in a breathless tone.

"Let's start with the good news. There's no sign of any sexual assault," he said and I watched both of Carly's parents heave a sigh of relief. The doctor cleared his throat. "But there's no sign of any drugs in her system that would account for the memory loss."

"Most drugs that cause memory loss metabolize quickly. They wouldn't show up in blood tests at this point," Molly interrupted.

"Which is why we can't say for certain they're the culprit. We'd like to run more tests to rule out any sort of head trauma."

"Whatever you think is necessary," Mr. Ramirez answered, pulling his wife into a tight embrace.

The doctor gave Molly and I a curt nod before disappearing down the hallway to see his next patient. My mind was already spinning, trying to fit pieces together that didn't quite make sense. I didn't think the Order was stupid enough to use drugs. If they gave her too much or didn't wait long enough after they let her go—assuming she hadn't escaped on her own—then it would show up. Drugs could be traced and the trail always led back to both the supplier and buyer. No, if they'd messed with her memory, it was done with magic.

"What's going on in that head of yours?" Molly sounded remarkably like Jacquie.

"They aren't going to find any drugs, because the people who took Carly and the other girls are smart enough to know those could be traced back to them."

"So, what are you saying?"

"They used what they had available to them ... Dark magic."

"Okay. And how exactly does knowing that help us?"

I grinned, a plan forming as I turned to look at the agent beside me. "Because I know a guy who can help."

TWENTY-FOUR

"Where are we going, exactly?" Molly asked once we were in the parking lot.

"I told you, to get someone who can help. Someone we can trust," I replied, my steps picking up pace as a sense of excitement electrified the rest of my body. Not only did I have complete confidence in the skills of the person we were headed to see, but I knew the Solstice would give us an extra boost too.

"Right, but who is it?" She called, picking up her pace to fall back into step with me.

"You'll see," I replied and climbed behind the wheel.

The trip back to the precinct didn't take nearly as long as I had expected. I caught sight of Jacquie in the bullpen, but she was too engrossed with whatever was on her computer to notice us. Molly grabbed my arm as I headed up to the second floor.

"Your partner, how did she handle learning about all this ... stuff?"

"You'd have to ask her. Like I said before, she already knew everything before we were even partners."

"I'll do that," she murmured and released her grip on my arm.

I led her up the stairs to Desmond's office. I saw light beneath the door, but didn't hear voices in conversation like I had last time. Good. I needed Des focused on what I was about to ask of him.

"The department's psychologist is going to help with a magical problem?" Molly hissed.

I flashed her a smile. "Oh, I didn't tell you? He's my cousin."

I let that sink in for a minute and gave a short knock on the door. Footsteps echoed from within and Desmond appeared moments later as realization dawned on the agent's face.

"You visiting twice in as many days and it's not even department mandated," he quipped before spotting Molly. "Good afternoon, Agent ..."

"Cartwright," she answered in a raspy tone.

"She knows," I said curtly and walked in. We didn't have time to stand around in doorways ogling each other.

"How much?" Desmond directed the question my way.

"Magic is a real thing and apparently you have it," Molly answered.

"Would you give us just a minute?" Desmond asked. By the forced smile on his lips, I knew he was about to lose his temper with me.

"Yell at me for breaking secrecy later. We're here, because we need your help," I said, waving Molly into the room.

Desmond took a slow breath before returning to sit behind his desk. Our topic of conversation may not be for all ears, but if anyone stumbled in, it would at least look department official. "How can I help?"

"I'm assuming you heard they found Carly Ramirez wandering on the Common today," I began.

"I had. How is she?"

"Missing a chunk of her memory," I replied.

Des rubbed the reddish-brown stubble on his chin, his gaze flitting between Molly and I. "Have the doctors ruled out drugs?"

"For now, they think so," Molly said, crossing her arms over her chest. "Ezri here thinks it was ... dark magic."

"Our kidnapper is with the Order, even if she's low-level. They wouldn't be dumb enough to use something that's easily traced back to them. Especially something as mundane as drugs. So, I figured they had to use magic. Lucky for us we've got someone whose expertise is in magical memory recovery," I explained.

It was Molly's turn to look between Desmond and I. Her expression was less cautious curiosity and more 'this shit can't be real'. Looking much like she'd done when I dropped the magic truth bomb on her at Notre Dame, she doubled over laughing. Desmond was halfway out of his seat when I gestured for him to stay where he was.

"This is kind of her go-to reaction," I offered.

"Do I want to know why or how you brought a normal person ... from the FBI in on our family history?" He demanded as Molly continued to laugh beside me.

"I was interrogating a suspect. Her friends didn't appreciate me showing up and calling them out. So, they started throwing fireballs at me and Agent Cartwright showed up. It was kind of a cat-out-of-the-bag situation at that point."

"I'm sorry it's just ... almost perfect that a department psychologist deals with memories," Molly gasped, wiping at her eyes again. She cleared her throat and sat up straighter "I'm also sorry ... that isn't funny."

"People react to the revelation in different ways. At least you've got a healthy way of dealing." He turned his attention back to me. "Now, about your victim with memory loss. You want me to talk to her and see whether we can bring back any of her memories."

"Exactly." I was already on my feet.

"Uh ... just out of professional curiosity, how do you know it will work?" Molly was on her feet, too.

"Because Desmond helped me remember Taggart stabbing me and leaving me for dead," I said cheerily.

"Trust me, she wasn't so happy about that revelation when it happened. We weren't in a good place," Desmond added.

"Now I gotta hear the rest of that story," Molly said, flashing me a grin.

"Some other time. Right now, we've got a little girl to help."

I WAS grateful Captain Beech hadn't questioned our decision to bring Desmond in on the case. How to explain what he was going to do with Carly was a worry for a later time. Our trio traipsed back down the hallway at the hospital a half hour later to find Carly resting. She looked less worn out now that she'd been given some food and fluids. However, the haunted, lost look in her eyes remained.

"Hi, Carly. I'm Desmond. Do you recognize me?" He sat beside the bed, a notepad and pen in hand.

Carly's gaze flicked over her parents' faces before moving to me and then settling on Molly. I took a breath and approached the bed. "It's okay, Carly. Agent Cartwright knows about what we can do."

To that end, we didn't need the uniform listening in or even worse catching sight of any magic. It meant I needed to do a little of my own casting to give us a little privacy. Desmond opened his mouth to speak when I held up a finger to silence him.

"Just give me a minute." I gestured to my badge and the door to get my concern across to him. He nodded without saying a word and settled back in the chair.

"What are you doing?" Molly whispered.

"Giving us a little privacy," I replied and pressed my hands to the door. My magic snapped to attention thanks to the Solstice. It was eager to obey my needs and I couldn't hide the smile that appeared on my lips. Fresh strawberries nearly bowled me over as power poured out of my fingers. It slid over my skin like water, covering the door the moment the thought 'give us privacy' popped into my head.

"Does anyone else smell fruit?" Molly asked, looking around the room.

Mundane people can't sense magic. *Was I wrong about her?* I diverted a sliver of attention to probe the federal agent, but there was no hint of magic. Could the weight and strength of my magic be enough that people with no abilities could sense it?

I stepped back from the door, but my intent was clear. Until I released it, the spell would hold and we would be in our own private little bubble. Doctors and nurses wouldn't come to check on us—then again that wasn't all down to magic. We'd let Carly's doctor know we needed a little time with her.

"That would be my magic. I may have gone a little overboard," I said with a shrug.

"Get ready to smell some more and probably not all of it pleasant," Desmond muttered and addressed Carly again. "So, now that we are in private, do you recognize me?"

"You're on the Council," she answered.

"That's right. I also work with the police. I help people remember things they don't think they can. Would it be okay if I tried to help you remember what happened to you?"

Carly picked at the swatch of medical tape securing the IV in her left hand. "What if it's bad? What if I don't want to remember it? Can you take it away again?"

Desmond exhaled and leaned over to place a gentle hand on her arm. "No, but I can help you find ways to deal with it so it isn't so scary."

She glanced at her parents who nodded their consent before turning her attention back to Desmond. "Okay. I can try."

"Not to be the ignorant neophyte in the room, but what exactly is about to happen and how are we going to explain it to people who have no clue magic is real?" Molly interrupted.

"I don't know how to explain it exactly, but I might be able to show you," I answered.

"Ez, are you sure about that?"

"Why not? I'm stronger than I look, remember? Plus, the boost from today won't hurt."

"I don't usually have … passengers along for the ride. It could influence any memories she does recover. We can't have either of you asking questions along the way."

"Des, I promise we will be silent observers. Nothing more."

"That better be all you are."

I moved to stand behind Desmond and Molly took up residence on his other side. I gave Molly a confident smirk—masking that I had no idea if this was going to work—and waited for Desmond to begin. I assumed it made sense to let him get his techniques underway before we jumped onboard.

"Carly, I want you to close your eyes for me and think back to two days ago. Focus on the first thing that comes to mind about that day."

Carly's face scrunched up and then relaxed a little. "Mami let me go to the store for a special dinner."

"Great. I need you to just think about it, picture it in your mind. Can you do that?" The subtle hint of spearmint permeated the air, mixing with the potent taste of my own magic lingering on the doorframe.

"Okay," Carly murmured, settling back against her pillows.

"This is fascinating," Molly breathed.

"Shh," I hissed before taking her wrist in my left hand and placing my right on Des's shoulder.

"I can see it," Carly mumbled.

"I want you to fast forward through your day. You went out for groceries and where did you go? Show us," Desmond's voice softened as the scent of his magic intensified.

I waited a few beats before pouring my own magic back into the mix. I felt Desmond's response, blocking against my intrusion. I pushed harder, urging him to let down his barriers just a little so we could slip inside and catch a glimpse of what lay within Carly's mind.

"Stop fighting me," I hissed, pressing down on his shoulder for emphasis.

"I'm trying," he answered, his voice tight.

Slowly, so slowly, his magic lost its hardened edge, turning more liquid and malleable. It wasn't happy about the ride-along, but it let me slip in. I clamped my hand more firmly around Molly's wrist, trying to convince Des' magic that she was merely an extension of *my* own magic. His magic wasn't stupid. It recognized me as blood and maybe the stronger power, but it knew she wasn't like us and obviously didn't belong.

"Des, this isn't working," I huffed.

He blindly reached out a hand behind him in Molly's direction. "Give me your hand."

She did as she was told without asking questions. With two points of contact—one on each end of the spell—it didn't fight any more. It let her step into the magic, tolerating her presence.

Piece by piece the hospital room faded as Carly pulled us into her memory of the day she was taken. Memory Carly bounded up the stairs at Park Street, not a care in the world. Clearly unaware of the danger lurking behind her. I spotted the back of Lola's hand as she crested the stairs and shouldered her way past a family out into the summer air. Carly had her phone pressed to her ear.

"Mami, I know. I wrote it down on my phone," she said, reassuring her mother about something, probably the grocery list.

I watched as Lola stepped up next to Carly on the sidewalk. Memory Carly was still unaware of her abductor's close proximity. Then, I watched as Lola's hand flickered out of existence, pulling Carly into the invisible void with it.

"How did she do that?" Molly's voice broke the memory and we were back in the hospital room.

Desmond turned in his chair, fixing her with a glare that no doubt mirrored my own. Molly shrunk back, pulling her hands free of our grasps.

"Sorry. I just ... wasn't expecting her to vanish. I mean, I know I watched the surveillance tapes and that's what it looked like happened, but it didn't make sense."

"I thought you understood you were there to observe, not make commentary" Desmond snapped.

"I didn't mean to interrupt. I didn't realize I could." Embarrassment turned her cheeks pale and she took another shuffle backward. "I'll just let you two do your thing."

I squeezed Desmond's shoulder in sympathy this time, hoping it would also refocus him on the task at hand. He turned back to face Carly who lay in the bed, eyes still closed. Maybe the soothing touch of my cousin's magic had kept her under his influence.

"Let's try this again," he murmured.

Getting back into Carly's memory was easier without having to convince the magical energies around us to let Molly tag along. We found Carly disappearing under Lola's touch.

"Carly, do you see the woman who just touched you?" Desmond's voice came from a million miles off.

Memory Carly reappeared and turned to look at the spot where I stood. "What woman?"

I could see why Molly had been so quick to ask questions. Being a passive observer was not my strength either. I wanted to jump in and help guide Carly, but that was the whole reason I'd brought Desmond into this. He knew how to do this. He'd trained for it. Me, I just flung magic around and got lucky most of the time.

"There is a woman next to you on the street. Do you remember her?"

Carly's brow furrowed and she shook her head. "No."

Spearmint erupted all around us, pushing Carly harder to remember. All Memory Carly did was stand there staring at me in confused silence. It was like she wanted to remember, but there was nothing there to recall. I exerted a little of my own will, just enough to disrupt Desmond's grasp on things and pulled us back to the hospital room.

"You can't give up that quickly. This takes time," he said, rounding on me.

"I know, Des. I know. But I have an idea I wanted to run by you. Let me go in. Show me how to be there with her. Once I'm in, I just need you to keep Carly calm while I poke around."

"Poke around for what?" His gaze narrowed.

"Signs of dark magic. Remember with the security footage three months ago? I was able to pull apart the spell, unravel it. If there's dark magic keeping her memories locked up, then maybe I can do the same thing again. Let's face it. We don't have a ton of options or time. They may have let Carly go, but that doesn't mean they will be so considerate of Neveah and Gabby."

It turned my stomach to think of anything the

Order did as 'considerate.' Still, they'd returned her to her family. Either they weren't as terrible as I'd thought—I couldn't handle that being the case—or whatever prompted them to take her in the first place hadn't panned out.

"What about Neveah and Gabby?" Carly's voice was small, coming out in a squeak of air.

"We are looking for your friends. They went missing right after you did," I replied. She may be a child, but she wasn't stupid. She'd pick up on it if I tried to lie or sugar coat it.

"You think whatever happened to me, happened to them, too?"

"We think so, which is why we are trying to help you remember where you've been. So maybe we can find your friends faster and get them home to their families," I replied.

She sat up a little straighter in the bed and some of the confusion ebbed from her face. "I want to try it again. I want to remember, even if it's scary."

Brave kid. Her parents remained silent on the other side of the room, huddled together as they watched us work. I couldn't imagine being in their shoes, both longing for their child to remember and being terrified of what that memory might hold. After we pulled it out of wherever the Order had locked it away, they'd be left to deal with the fallout. Sure, Desmond would be around to help give her coping strategies. Still she'd never be able to put it back in the box and if she tried, it could backfire on her. Backfired magic never ends well. No matter what Kayla might say otherwise.

I stepped back up to the bed, placing my hand just below Desmond's on Carly's forearm. "This isn't going to hurt," I said. If anything, I'd be the one coming out with very real bruises if the magic decided to fight back.

"Okay," she said, pressing her lips together in a thin line. Her eyes fluttered shut and I sensed Des' magic, lulling her back into the memory. It tugged me in, too.

I found myself standing behind Carly at the crosswalk by Park Street. I could hear Desmond's voice telling Carly to just stay calm and ignore me. I looked around, trying to pinpoint anything that might be the root of the magic messing with her memory. Nothing seemed obvious not even the memory of Lola. That alone gave me an idea.

I closed my eyes, held my hands palms out and let my magic become the predominant sense. I touched the strands of energy that made up Carly's thoughts, buttressed by Desmond's familiar magic. Nothing off there. I turned clockwise until I was roughly lined up with Lola's figure. It felt uninviting, but not *wrong*. Since the magic had actually been done to Carly in the real world, it was *supposed* to exist in the memory.

"What doesn't belong?" I asked myself, taking a

step back from the scene. I tried to remember every-thing I could about the scene, sorting out details that made sense and ones that didn't. They had to have left a trail somewhere.

I opened my eyes again and looked at the scene. It had frozen—maybe Desmond's doing—and that was enough to tickle the tiny hairs on the nape of my neck. The sensation of being watched sent shivers down my back and I turned to see a home-less man. He had unkempt hair, dressed in baggy pants and an overcoat leering at me. It was summer, well over eighty degrees. No one would be in an overcoat. I took a step forward and he took one back. I spotted a small carrying case hanging from his belt.

"Gotcha," I said and took off after him.

He darted around trees and up the paths of the Common, making a break for the far end. I held out a hand, and an actual rope shot from my fingers, looping around his feet and dragging him to the ground. He thrashed against the rope, the binds leaving tiny marks in his flesh. Drawing dark, black blood that looked eerily similar to the magical computer virus I'd fought in March. It may not be the same spell, but it was similar enough to tell me it was the piece that didn't fit.

"You don't belong here," I said, settling my foot on his chest.

"Neither do you." The homeless man turned into

a pool of shadows, slipping free of my ropes and slithering away.

"Not a chance in hell," I snapped, erecting walls around the shadow that reached to the top of the tree line, blocking out the sun and denying it an exit skyward.

The sound of crunching stone filled my ears as the walls I'd erected crumbled to dust. The man standing in the middle of the debris resembled the homeless man except he now wore a tactical vest and a sidearm holstered at his hip. *Seriously, what is this thing?* At least when I was fighting the magical computer virus, it had the decency to stay in one form.

"Bring it," I said, motioning for him to come at me.

"As you wish," he said and charged.

Our bodies collided and I swear he had more mass than someone his size logically should have. Breath went out of my lungs and dark spots popped in my vision as I tried to take in oxygen. Mr. Tactical swung and I was too slow to dodge the blow, my jaw erupting in pain as I staggered back, leaving scuff marks in the gravel from the walls he'd destroyed.

"Not nice," I said, blood dripping down my chin.

"Give up," he called, as if he were being nice.

"Not a chance, asshole." I ran at him and landed a few punches myself. They barely left him with discolored skin. *So not fair!* I knew the pain in my jaw wasn't real, at least it shouldn't be. My knuckles ached from the blows I'd struck and I had to back pedal when he pulled the gun from his holster, leveling it at me.

"I will give you one final chance to surrender," he said coolly.

Since when did the Order let people surrender? "Fuck you."

"Goodbye, witch," he quipped and fired.

I'm not faster than a speeding bullet. Not by a long shot, but I still managed to turn the flying projectile into grains of dust before it hit me. My opponent looked pissed, but not defeated.

"You better have some luck soon, Ez. I can't keep this up for much longer," Desmond's voice filled all the available space around me.

"Working on it," I answered through the pain and charged the man one final time. The case I'd noticed on his hobo form had transformed into a belt buckle. Well, sometimes, you just gotta pants a guy.

I don't think he expected me to tackle him again. Not after disintegrating his bullet. We both went down hard. This time his mass vanished and became more figment than I was. I felt the gravel beneath my hands bite into the sensitive flesh of my palms. I ignored the additional pain, instead clawing at him, trying to get my hands around the belt buckle. I wasn't sure what exactly it was, but I could feel it was important. After all, every box with a lock had a key. My fingers brushed against the cool metal of the buckle and a jolt of pain zipped up my arm, lighting every nerve ending on fire.

"Fuck!" I rolled off him, cradling my arm. There didn't appear to be any outward damage, but who knew what was going on internally. For all I knew it could sense the light magic in me and was repelling me like a bug zapper. So, I needed to get creative. An idea—a terrible idea that probably wouldn't work and could leave me literally petrified—formed. "Please don't let this be the worst idea ever."

I turned my magic inward, to the tiny ball of stone that was Taggart's magic. It had lain dormant for months, only recently awakening to try and kill me. Now though, I begged it to come out to play. To wrap itself around my hands and arms, to give me not only the strength and stone skin of a gargoyle, but the taint of his dark magic. The smell of his magic nauseated me and I nearly stopped. My magic pummeled me, trying to fight off the spell. *Relax and let it happen.*

"You are not alone," a now-familiar voice said in my ear.

I didn't look, but I felt Theodora's hand on my shoulder, lending me her strength. I looked down at my hands and found they'd turned to stone. I advanced on the manifestation of dark magic and yanked the belt buckle free. It sat like a lump in my palm until it shimmered and reformed into a tiny vial of silver liquid.

"The child needs it," Theodora said.

In the blink of an eye I was back with memory Carly. My hands were still made of stone and I could feel it trying to move past my elbows and root itself deep inside of me.

"Des, you need to tell Carly she needs to take the vial I'm about to hand her and drink it," I said through gritted teeth.

"Carly, I know this is going to sound strange, but I need you to take what Ezri is about to give you. See it in your mind and drink it," Desmond's voice instructed.

Memory Carly gazed up at me with confusion on her face, but she took the vial I held out to her. She pressed it to her lips—having to explain to a ten-year-old how she was able to alter things in her own memory was going to be fun—and the liquid disappeared. Once gone, everything changed.

Images, sounds, smells all flashed by like a video on fast forward. Whatever the Order had locked in her head was flooding back. The ground beneath my feet began to rumble and split open. Her memory of the abduction was shattering or it was all just too much for her young mind to handle all at once. Suddenly, everything took on a haze and spearmint permeated my senses. It clung to my nose and stuck down my throat. Desmond was doing what he could to keep her calm.

I needed to get out of this. I looked down at my hands and was greeted with rough stone. I needed to find a way to suppress Taggart's magic now that I no longer had need of it. Despite being covered in granite my hands still shook as I tried to summon my own magic. It fizzled and crackled along the rough-hewn layers of skin, but did little else.

"Come on. You know how to fight this," I muttered and closed my eyes, focusing on the image of the stone receding from my body, curling up into the little nugget of darkness I carried around inside me.

"Ezri!" Molly's voice bellowed in my ear.

I cracked one lid open to find myself back in the hospital room. Carly was slumped against the pillows beneath her, clearly worn out. Enjoying a little magical-induced sleep courtesy of Desmond.

"What happened to you?" Mrs. Ramirez rasped, gesturing to my hands.

I glanced down and my whole body went cold. The stone hadn't receded since it already existed in my body. It made sense for it to manifest in the real world too. Molly tentatively prodded at the roughness of my left forearm.

"I don't know whether to think that's really cool or scary as shit." She blushed and looked at Carly.

"It's definitely not cool," Desmond said, the skin

around his eyes pinched with worry. He'd been there when I'd pulled the magic out of Kevin and saw first-hand what it had done to me.

"I'll be fine," I coughed trying not to move despite the agony in my chest.

I focused on flexing my fingers, urging them to become flesh and bone again. Slowly, grain by grain the stone receded, leaving behind pale flesh. My hands and arms ached the moment it was gone. I leaned back in the chair and winced at a new pain in my left flank. I reached down and felt something protruding.

"You need a doctor," Molly said, starting for the door.

"No. I need a Healer," I wheezed.

"What's the difference?" She huffed.

"Healers don't ask questions she can't answer. She walked into this hospital with no injuries and as far as anyone knows, she hasn't left this room. How would you explain a sudden rib fracture and facial bruising?" Desmond answered, pressing the tips of his fingers to the unnatural bump in my side. "I can't do much." I probed my jaw and winced at the tenderness.

"Let me try," Mr. Ramirez said, leaving his wife's side for the first time since we'd arrived.

I nodded, my breathing becoming harder the longer my rib continued to jut out at an unnatural angle. Mr. Ramirez placed his hand on my side and I sensed the tangy taste of citrus on my tongue. It tasted like grapefruit. *Interesting.* I reminded my body that he was just trying to help and my magic thankfully obeyed. The rib throbbed in agony with jolts of white-hot pain until it abruptly dulled and I could breathe easier. "Thanks."

"You brought our baby home. How could I not offer my help?"

Still I hadn't really done anything to get Carly home. If I was being brutally honest with myself, my bringing Desmond in had just opened the floodgates and Carly was in for a long road of recovery.

"Did you find what you needed?" Mrs. Ramirez asked in a hoarse tone.

"We helped Carly start to remember. It's going to take more time for her memory to come fully back. For now though, we need to let her rest," Desmond answered.

I took that as my cue to get up and release the spell on the doorway. I expected the magic to just fade back into the world, becoming energy for anyone else to use. Instead, it slithered back into my palms, pooling there in translucent puddles before seeping back into my pores. Guess I must have needed the magical boost.

"We'll be in touch," I addressed Carly's parents before leading Desmond and Molly out of the room.

We made it to the parking lot before Molly got in front of me, barring my path forward. "What did you do with the stone thing? And why did you look so freaked out when it happened?" She pointed between me and Desmond.

"Here's not the best place to discuss this. Why don't we go back to my office?" Desmond responded.

DESPITE THE SITUATION, Desmond's office felt cozy and safe. I'd found my family again in this room, shared fears and secrets within its walls. It hadn't always been that way. For a long time, I'd associated it with pain, grief, and danger. I wondered when it had made the transition. Des and I stared back at each other while Molly paced off to the side.

"Okay, so what happened back there?" Molly demanded.

"I'd like to know the answer, too," Desmond added in a less accusatory tone.

"I was able to find the dark magic keeping hold of Carly's memory. It was a homeless man oddly enough ... well, sort of. Anyway, we got into it and I realized he was protecting a key. I tried to grab it, but it nearly fried me." I flexed my fingers at the memory. They still ached. "That's when I realized they'd put in a failsafe against light magic."

"You could have lost control. It could have killed you!" Desmond railed.

"I know," I lowered my gaze. "What other choice did I have?"

"It's cute how you two are on the same page and can talk all cryptically, but I have no idea what you're talking about," Molly reminded us.

"Taggart used dark magic to turn a kid's own magic inward on himself. It made him a gargoyle. I freed him, but magic can't be destroyed ... Not really. It always exists in the world. This spell needed to bind to someone and so it bound itself to me. If I'm not careful, it can take hold, turning my own magic against me until I'm a stone statue. Somehow it worked and I was able to trick the magic in Carly's head into thinking I was evil, too." I fixed Desmond with a withering look as he opened his mouth. "Don't worry, I'm fine."

"Jesus," Molly rubbed her temples. "I'm starting to regret asking for the answer. This is all just a lot to take in."

"Which is why we usually keep the existence of magic quiet," Desmond stated pointedly looking at me.

"I'm guessing you can't really put the toothpaste back in this particular tube." She gave a small half smile and tugged a few loose strands of hair out of her face.

"Nope," I said, stifling a yawn. Even with the boost from the Solstice, tapping into Taggart's magic had worn me out.

"You said it worked though. You got her to remember." She changed tracks.

"Sort of. Tons of memories flooded her subconscious. It hit her all at once, but things are bound to be jumbled," I said.

"It's why I put her into somewhat of a coma. She needs time to sort through things."

"But the other girls don't have time," Molly protested.

"I know, but if we try to push her, we could do more damage than they did," Des said. The pinched look that had overtaken him at the sight of me turning to stone hadn't lifted despite my return to the flesh and bone club.

"We might have a way to figure out what she's not able to tell us right now, though," I said, another foolish idea taking root in my brain.

"We do?" Desmond and Molly questioned in unison.

"I saw everything that was flashing by in her head. It's simple. we just have Desmond go back into *my* memory and we can sort through it," I said, trying to give them a 'piece-of-cake' smile.

"I've never done that before, Ez," Desmond murmured.

"Come on, cuz. You are just as much a badass as I am. I believe in you and we've got the best signal booster we could ask for." I gestured to the wall calendar hanging on the door behind me.

"The Solstice makes us stronger, but it isn't limitless."

"We're not asking it to be limitless. We just need it to stretch a little more for us." Besides, I had an idea of how I could make things easier on my end. He just didn't need to know about my connection to our ancestors. For all the support Desmond offered me now, I knew he'd spent a lot of his youth envying me for my role as Savior. Hell, he'd told me that he wished he could have taken the burden from me when I was a teenager. Back before my mother's death drove a wedge between us.

"Fine. If you think it's worth trying. Go for it. But I want in this time. I will be quiet and not ask any questions. I swear," Molly said, arms crossed over her chest.

"We aren't doing it here. If we do this, and I'm still not convinced it's a good idea, we are doing it where there are Healers around."

Time to introduce Molly to the Authority.

TWENTY-FIVE

The atmosphere at headquarters was thick with tension as I led Molly into the foyer. It wasn't nearly bustling like usual, even with it being mid-afternoon. I just had to hope there were Healers around. I would prefer J.T., even if it meant he'd be peppering me with questions about whatever magical injuries I sustained. My wish came true as my boyfriend descended the stairs from the second floor.

"Hey, you," he said, pulling me into a tight embrace and a kiss before realizing I had an entourage.

"Her boyfriend," Desmond stage whispered.

"Des, surprised to see you here during department work hours. Whatever's going on must be serious," J.T. said.

"Blame your girlfriend," he retorted, his skepticism about what I was planning coming through as irritation.

"I'm glad you're here," I addressed J.T., trying to diffuse the tension. "We're going to need you." I started up the stairs past him.

"That's not ominous or anything," J.T. said, but was on my heels half a second later.

I glanced over my shoulder long enough to see Molly follow J.T. and Desmond bringing up the rear. Molly's head swiveled side to side as she took in the architecture and the sheer vastness that the building exuded.

"This is the Authority?" She murmured.

JT and I reached the landing first. He leaned in to whisper in my ear. "Who's the newbie?"

"Special Agent Molly Cartwright, FBI. She sort of stumbled into our world."

"With a little assist from my favorite Savior?" He quipped.

"Well when you get caught in the middle of a fire fight with actual fireballs, it's a little hard to lie," I said and stepped into the Council chamber.

"To answer your question," J.T. began and whirled to usher Molly inside. "The Authority is the organization. This is just our HQ."

"It's beautiful," she whispered.

Desmond was last into the room and eased the door shut. J.T. took a few steps closer to my cousin. "So, what am I blaming Ezri for?"

"She has some crazy plan and honestly, I'm not sure it's going to work. Plus, it's dangerous," Desmond answered.

I settled in one of the chairs near the center of the semicircle and waited for the rest of them to join me. "We're wasting time," I noted when no one else moved.

"Are you really sure you want to do this?" Desmond pressed.

"Want? Hell no, but I need to do it ... because I've still got two little girls depending on me." Besides if I was lucky and Adrian was somehow involved in this mess, maybe finding Gabby and Neveah would give me some answers about his whereabouts.

Desmond wet his lips, glanced at the two others in the room and pointed to me. "Lay down across the chairs. It's going to be more comfortable that way.

I wasn't sure my comfort was really an issue. Still if it made him feel better about it, I'd do it. I pushed the chairs into a straight line and settled across three of them, saying a silent thanks that the seats were padded with soft cushions. Molly hovered near my head until the chair directly above my head creaked and she sat down. J.T. settled near the end of the group of chairs and Desmond pulled one around to sit beside me.

"If you can, I'd try to clear all the other magic from your system," Desmond began.

Nodding while lying flat was kind of impossible so I gave my cousin a thumbs up. I pressed my fingers to the sandalwood charm at my throat and inhaled deeply. The scent of his and Mr. Ramirez's magic washed away. The grimy feeling of tapping into Taggart's magic faded, too, and I sighed with relief. Just to be sure I was in control, I let a little power leak out into the room around us, cooling things off with the hint of berries.

"I'm ready," I said.

"I'm going to remind you that I've never done this before so if shit goes sideways, don't blame me," Desmond said, clasping my left hand in one of his own.

"I understand, Des." I reached my free arm back up over my head. "If you're coming along for the ride, you're going to need two touch points," I addressed Molly.

"Oh, right. And before either of you say it, I know, just shut up and watch."

"Okay, Ez, I need you to focus on the point in your memory right before everything hit you. We need a stable place to start," Desmond said.

I did my best to settle against the cushions and recall the image of Carly about to sip from the vial that had unlocked her memories. The heady scent of my cousin's magic wrapped around me like a blanket and I sunk into its familiarity. The less I fought his intent, the easier this would be. For a split second a different memory flickered to the surface: one of me lying prone and bloody on a sidewalk, knife sticking out of my gut. I gritted my teeth and pushed that memory back into the recesses of my mind.

The image around me changed to Park Street. Carly stood in front of me, the semi-invisible form of Lola at her side. The vial was paused partway to the girl's lips.

"Okay, I'm here," I said. I glanced over my shoulder to see Molly standing by one of the pretzel carts. She mimed zipping her lips.

"I want you to let the memory play out. Don't try to manipulate it at all. Just let it come," Desmond's voice prompted.

I swallowed, watching the memory play out. The scenery shifted rapid fire as memories whizzed by. I wasn't covered in stone this time, even though I occupied the same space I had in Carly's memory. *Thank God for small mercies.* The physicality of moving through memory is weird.

"I'm going to try rewinding and slowing things down," I said to the air around me, assuming Desmond would get the message.

I heard a sound like a cough behind me, but didn't bother to acknowledge Molly. I didn't need her distraction. Holding my hands out at my sides, I rewound the memory. Sights and sounds flew by in reverse, even more garbled than when they'd first appeared. I halted it just before it disappeared altogether.

Show it to me slower. Strawberries bloomed all around me, shooting out of my hands like ropes, tethering me to the memory. I hadn't expected that to happen, but then again, I'd never played with someone else's memories. In an odd way it made sense that I'd need a link of some kind to keep control and make the memories obey me. I also needed the memories to not be so all encompassing. Using the connection of my magic, I shrunk the images into something that might fit on a flat screen TV. Making the process much more manageable.

As interesting as it might be to watch in detail how Lola convinced Carly to go with her—and I would be revisiting that encounter—I needed to know where Lola had taken Carly and what had been done to her there. Flicking my finger as if I were using a touch screen, I moved through snippets of memory. Scanning them and trying to find anything I could about their destination, but the scenery was all a blur.

"Desmond, I need to see the surroundings more clearly. Can you do anything to help me out?" I called.

"I'll try," he replied and strands of spearmint twisted into the strawberry ropes, feeding more magic into the spell.

Unfortunately, even with Des' signal boost, the

imagery was still too blurry to make out any discernable landmarks. Letting out an annoyed grunt, I flicked forward through the memories, hoping for a destination. The images around me resolved into a dark room and the strong scent of brackish water assaulted my nose. Lola must have done something that left the scent of her magic behind for a long time. I took time to examine the room. It was nondescript with only one way in and out. I needed a better look and with a flick of my wrist the image leapt off my memory screen to fill the available space around me until I stood at the center of the room. I paced the perimeter of the room. The walls felt slick like metal. I had a good enough vantage point thanks to Carly and noticed a small cot in one corner.

"They kept her in a little room somewhere. Lola must have done something to her, because it stinks of her magic," I narrated, even though Molly—who was really the only other person who needed to be able to see it—could see what I saw.

"That's progress," Desmond said. He sounded tired.

I turned and caught Molly waving her arms frantically at me. She wanted to speak, but probably didn't want a repeat of what happened at the hospital. I sighed and nodded. "What's up?"

"Can you see if she interacted with anyone besides Lola?"

"That's what I was about to do," I noted.

Molly gave a thumbs up and stepped back. Shrinking the memory of the room down to the size of the flat screen was easier the second time. I flicked forward through the images that came after the room, but they didn't make sense. In the next image Carly was standing on the Common in afternoon light. The one after it showed her being held down by hazy figures whose magic stunk the same as the homeless man that had been guarding his treasure trove.

"Shit." They were out of order, jumbled likely on purpose. So even if we managed to recover them, they'd make no damn sense, and we'd only be spinning our wheels trying to work our way through them. It wasn't like I could just give them to Avery on a flash drive to sort through.

The images continued to play, but went dark, only conveying sounds and voices. I heard a deep male voice say "She's not the one. Get rid of her." I didn't like his tone, like he thought Carly was nothing more than trash to be discarded. The darkness continued and this time my throat tightened as a child's screams filled the air around me—Carly's screams. For a brief moment I was grateful these weren't my memories so I wouldn't have to relive whatever pain she was enduring.

"I don't know. I don't know. I can't see anything. I promise," Carly wailed.

"Don't lie. You have the gift in your blood. Now,

tell me what's on the horizon," the same male voice demanded.

"I can't," she whimpered.

I paused the memories and clutched at my chest. The Order had targeted her for her bloodline. The fact that at least one of the girls had the possibility of foresight was starting to make more sense.

I pulled my magic back from the memories, breaking my link to them. They faded, replaced by that damn memory of nearly dying. I gasped, coming back to reality in the Council room. I released my grip on Molly's hand and sat up. My stomach muscles twinged, remembering the feel of the blade piercing flesh and muscle.

"It's her bloodline," I said, trying to calm my racing pulse.

J.T. appeared at my side, pressing a hand to my throat to check my heartrate. The sweet honey of his magic infused my body with every breath, calming me. As crazy magical investigating techniques went, this one had been far less fatal than I'd expected. Desmond looked worn out, dark circles were under his eyes and his usually rosy complexion was pale.

"If you don't mind, I need a break," Desmond said, excusing himself before I could object.

I made a mental note to check in with him later. I'd never seen memory work take such a toll on him. The Solstice should have taken any major edge off the spellcasting. I turned my attention back to Molly.

"They were trying to unlock something in Carly's blood."

"I heard. I don't know what that means."

"Magic is passed through blood and families have different gifts. J.T. here is a Healer and so is Adrian Baptiste. Or at least he will be when he turns eighteen."

"Our other missing kid who seems to be the link between the girls?"

"Maybe. I need to talk to Jacquie and Mrs. Freeman. I need to know if there's a possibility that they have certain magical family traits that might pique the Order's interest."

"You know, the more we dig, the more it looks like this Adrian kid might be involved. All three girls had contact with him. He was in a position to gain their trust. It looks really suspicious that he went missing around the same time."

I didn't disagree with her, but what's his motivation for helping the Order or putting lives in danger. "That may be so, but I have to believe if he was involved, it was unwitting. He was trying to reconnect with family. It's entirely possible the Order found out and used that to their advantage."

"I hope you're right. Still you should prepare yourself for that not being the case."

I didn't respond. I needed to stay focused on the girls. Bringing them back safe might just be the thing that could bring Adrian home, too.

TWENTY-SIX

After downing the glass of water J.T. had thrust into my hands, Molly and I left Desmond at headquarters. I knew I should check in with my cousin and see what was really going on. He'd do the same for me. *After this case is solved.*

"Is that a normal thing for you?" Molly questioned, breaking the silence in the car.

"Is what normal?" I kept my gaze on the road ahead of me.

"Whatever the hell it was you just did ... flip through someone else's memory like a movie. Fight shapeshifting bad guys."

"No, it's not what I'd call normal. Most of the cases Jacquie and I work are mundane, boring crimes. The ones with magic wrapped up in them are rare, but that usually makes them a lot more deadly."

Molly picked at the hem of her blouse as I rolled to a stop at a red light. I watched her and waited for her to speak. By the way her jaw was working, I knew she wanted to say something.

"What's the question?" I prompted.

"When all of this is over, what happens then?" She sounded so unsure of herself. Not at all like the agent I'd met in the conference room.

"What do you mean?" I had a suspicion about the root of the question, but I wanted to hear her say it.

"Do you wipe my memory of everything I've seen? So I go back to my life unaware of all the extra crazy shit happening around me?"

"No. First of all, messing with memories is tricky and dangerous. Just look at what happened to Carly. Second, I don't know if or when our paths will cross again. Still I have to keep reminding myself, having allies is a good thing. It means I don't have to do everything myself, despite what the whole savior moniker implies."

She relaxed in the seat just as the light turned green and I pressed down on the accelerator. "Okay, good. Because as bizarre as all of this is, in a way, it all makes perfect sense. Like I think a part of me has always kind of noticed strange things that don't quite fit with what everyone else says should be the case. Maybe I've always been sensitive to magic. Is that a thing? I don't know ... is that strange to say?"

I shrugged one shoulder. "You're asking the wrong person. Although I guess there must be people out there who aren't magical, but are more sensitive to it. Who have an easier time accepting the reality of it. Maybe we just got lucky and you're one of those people."

"Maybe," she said, turning her attention to the traffic whizzing by us.

Before I could say anything else, my phone buzzed in the center console with an incoming call from Jacquie. I swiped to accept the call and put it on speaker. "Hey, what's up?"

"Where are you?" Jacquie's voice was strained, like she hadn't slept in a while.

"On my way back to the precinct with Agent Cartwright. Why, what's going on?"

"We have a visitor."

Vague much? "Who?" After a beat I added, "You can talk openly. She knows about magic."

"Oh." A pause and then, "Adrian Baptiste's cousin is here. She says she needs to speak with both of us."

"She knows you're running lead on this case, right?" I answered.

"She's insisting that she speak with you, too."

Great. Like I don't already have enough to juggle. "Fine. Be there in ten."

Jacquie ended the call and Molly eyed me with a curious expression. "You talked to his cousin?"

"Well, yeah. He called her right after he ditched his phone at South Station. She insists she hasn't seen him and that she expected him to show up, but he never did. Either she's changing her story or by some miracle he's reached out again."

I hoped it was the latter. If I could just sit down with Adrian and talk to him, maybe I could understand how he fit into all of this. Honestly, he hadn't seemed like the type to lure kids into danger.

I pressed down on the gas, needing to get to our destination faster. I got a few angry horn honks as my speed surpassed the limit, but I didn't care. I pulled into a spot in the parking lot beside the precinct and was out of the car before the engine had time to settle. Molly was hot on my heels as I strode into the bullpen. Jacquie sat at her desk and Natalia Baptiste sat silently beside her. They both looked up at our approach.

"Why don't we go somewhere a little more private?" I said, locking eyes with Natalia.

"Sure." She stood, brushing strands of her dark hair over one shoulder.

Jacquie stood to follow us, stopping momentarily to address Molly, extending a hand. "Welcome to the club," she said softly.

Molly took Jacquie's outstretched hand and shook it. "When things settle down, I'll be wanting to pick your brain ... I'm sure."

My partner only nodded before falling into step beside me. "So, how'd that happen?"

"I'll fill you in later," I huffed, ushering Natalia into one of the interview rooms.

Jacquie shut the door behind us and we both settled into the side by side seats. Natalia looked at her hands, clearly a sign of nervousness. Maybe she was here to change her story.

"What was so important you had to tell me, when Detective DeWitt is the lead investigator on Adrian's case?" I leaned on the table.

"He called me again," she said, pulling out her phone and laying it on the table between us.

"When?" Jacquie and I demanded in unison.

"About an hour ago. He said he was sorry for bailing on me, but he'd found what he needed. He just wanted me to know everything was fine and that I shouldn't worry. But ... until you all showed up at my shop, I *wasn't* worried. Still the fact he called me and not his mother worries me even more."

"When he called you, could you hear any noises in the background that might give you some sense of where he might be calling from?" I pressed.

Natalia closed her eyes and after a moment shook her head. "No. Now that I think about it, it was very quiet. Eerily so on the other end. Even if he was inside somewhere there would be ambient noise, right?"

Only if there was anything to create noise. If he

was locked in a windowless room that might explain the absence of sound on his end. "Did he sound distressed, like someone was forcing him to tell you he was fine?"

"No. he sounded like he did when he called me the other day … when he didn't show up." She leaned across the table, forcing me and Jacquie to lean in to hear her. "The only thing I can think of is maybe he wasn't on this plane of existence."

"Sorry?" Jacquie arched a brow.

"The dead are a lot like the living, especially those with magic. They can manifest, especially if they've recently passed over. If he was holding his phone then he could have managed to call me."

"So you think Adrian's dead?" I said.

"Truly I hope he isn't, but it's the only thing I can think of that would explain the absence of sound around him."

"Let's not jump to conclusions, okay? Besides, given your skills wouldn't you know if he'd … passed over?" I pushed.

"If I'd been at the shop maybe, but I wasn't. I was getting a late lunch. I was out of the city. Look, I'm just telling you what this feels like. I hope I'm wrong. I just … I wasn't expecting to get pulled into family shit like this." The inflection in her tone conveyed there was more to the 'family shit' that she wasn't sharing. Maybe it wasn't relevant or maybe she didn't trust us enough yet to bring it up.

Jacquie nudged my foot under the table and I pushed my chair back. "Give us a minute."

We stepped into the hallway and I eased the door shut. "Well?"

"Dead people making phone calls from beyond the grave seems like a stretch," Jacquie said.

"That's my thought, too. We made some progress with Carly ... well sort of. Whatever, the point is, they were keeping her in a windowless room. It was pretty damn quiet in there. Like not even an air conditioner or vent to feed in air or any kind of noises. So maybe he was in a room like that devoid of sound."

"Definitely seems a lot more plausible. You think she's trying to throw us off, tell us he's dead so we stop looking for him?"

"Maybe. She did try to hide evidence from us before. Besides, I just don't buy that she suddenly had this estranged cousin fall into her lap. He's communicating with her via a burner phone when he could be reaching out to his mother who he has to know is worried about him. That's just suspicious as hell," I noted.

"Agreed. Let's cut her loose. I'll have an unmarked car sit on her and see if he shows up at her place."

"Good idea. I need to talk to Denise and Melissa Freeman again," I said.

"What did you find with Carly?"

"It's better I explain it with everyone together. I know I don't have a right to ask you this, but do you think you can keep Denise under control? I don't need her storming the hospital and traumatizing a little girl more than she already is."

"I'll do what I can. Where are we meeting?"

"Here is probably easiest. We can use the conference room." I took a step back toward the bullpen when she caught my arm.

"You want to fill me in on our new FBI friend?"

"Short version, she tailed me to Notre Dame when I went to have a chat with our kidnapper. Things got heated and she saw magic first hand. Couldn't put that genie back in the bottle so I figured it was easier to just bring her in on the secret. The Council can ream me out all they want when this is done."

"Let me guess, your excuse is going to be I'm the Savior?" She said with a small laugh.

"You know me well, partner."

The small signs of joviality vanished as her face turned stony and determined once more. "They didn't physically hurt Carly, right?" Her tone turned solemn and low.

"A few bruises, but nothing some pain meds won't cure." I rubbed the nape of my neck. "The bigger issue is her mind. They scrambled her head enough that it's going to take Desmond a long time to help her get right again." *Still that's only if he isn't spending that time sorting his own head out.*

"I can't decide if them letting her go is a good sign for the others or just a fluke," Jacquie sighed.

I shared her conflicted sentiment. The Order hadn't gotten what they needed from Carly. They could have killed her, but they let her go. I still didn't understand how a group who was ruthless enough to murder strangers had enough heart to let a child go. I squeezed Jacquie's shoulder. "I'm going to get them home, I promise. And I'm going to beat the ever-living shit out of some bad guys to do it, too."

"What have I told you about making promises, Rookie?" There was no sense of superiority as she said the last word, not like in the past.

"Yeah, well, you're the exception. However, the sooner we wrap up these cases the better. Agent Cartwright is nice and all, but she's no substitute for my partner. I miss having you watching my back."

"I've always got your back, Ezri. Even if you can't see me. Now, go do your job, Detective."

I left her standing in the hallway as I returned to my desk. Time for me to start digging into bloodlines. I hoped they held the answer that Carly's jumbled memories had been unable to provide.

I regretted the decision to meet with everyone at the precinct the moment Melissa Freeman and her little boy showed up. The conference room was hardly as private as we needed it to be and I doubted I could get away with a silencing spell again. For one thing, despite the brave face I put on, the close call with letting Taggart's magic out had taken more out of me than I wanted to admit. I wasn't sure I'd be able to sustain it, even with the boost of the Solstice.

"What's the matter?" Molly asked. She'd discarded her FBI windbreaker and had rolled up the sleeves of her shirt.

"Nothing," I lied eying the front desk as Denise and Troy appeared.

Jacquie met them at the reception desk and gestured to the conference room. I gave a small half-hearted wave at their approach before stepping aside to let them in.

"You aren't being honest," Molly whispered in my ear. "Something is the matter. I get it, we don't know each other that well. You don't have to share. Just tell me that it won't affect your ability to keep working this case."

"Can I offer you a piece of advice, Agent?" Jacquie stepped up to where we stood. She continued before Molly could object. "Questioning Ezri's objectivity in a case where magic is involved is a stupid move. Trust me, I've been where you are. I get you want to ensure the integrity of the case and protect her. She's a big girl and if she messes up, she'll own it."

I appreciated Jacquie's words—well maybe not the part about messing up—my partner buoyed me enough to face the two worried families in the conference room. Screw it if people overheard the topic of our discussion. It wasn't their case and they should just mind their own damn business.

Before I could step inside, the desk sergeant waved his hand to catch my attention and summoned me with a sharp wave of his fingers. Leaving Jacquie and Molly to stare awkwardly at each other, I crossed the bullpen. I saw a harried looking woman accompanied by a young man— barely older than our missing girls—sitting across from the desk.

"What's up, Sergeant?" I leaned on the desk, glancing back the way I'd come. I hoped my nervous energy and air of irritation conveyed how much I didn't appreciate the interruption.

"These folks said they're here to see a ... Lola Cox," the sergeant answered, pointing to the woman and boy.

Shit! I'd forgotten about the promise to Lola to let her see her little brother. I hadn't expected the social worker to agree so readily, especially given Lola was facing a lot of jail time. Probably enough that she wouldn't be out until well after her brother's eighteenth birthday—even with a deal. I breathed out through my nose as I turned to face the people waiting silently across from me.

"Hi, I'm Detective Trenton. We spoke a little while ago," I said, offering my hand to the woman.

"Yes." She looked to the young man. "Is there somewhere we could speak privately?"

"Of course. This way," I started to lead them both to an interview room, but I heard her tell the boy to stay put. The desk sergeant assured her he'd keep an eye on the kid.

"His sister, you said she's been arrested," the social worker began with a sigh.

"Yeah. She's a suspect in a few cases I'm working," I said, trying to be as vague as possible.

"I'll be honest, she aged out of the program a few years back and we haven't heard from her since. Not that I think she's able to support her little brother or is at all a good choice for a guardian. Still it seems suspicious that she gets arrested and now she wants to see him."

I paused to take in what she'd said. Her story didn't fit with what Lola had said. I'd gotten the impression the Order had been dangling her brother over her head as motivation to do their dirty work. She certainly hadn't denied it when I brought it up and she made it seem like she was on a crusade to get him back. Not that she had just tossed him aside. "I'll be honest, that doesn't fit with the information she provided to us when she asked us to arrange a meeting. It seemed she was trying to get in touch with him for quite some time."

"Unless they've been communicating under the radar which is unlikely given how strictly his foster parents monitor his phone and internet. She's leading you on, Detective. She's a compulsive liar. Going on about how they had special powers. She needed more help than we could give her."

I bristled at the woman's statement. She was clearly in the dark about the magical community which also explained a few things. For one, growing up in the foster care system and not realizing that magic was a part of you or having to hide it. That scenario could definitely lead to her magic turning on her and making her a Whisperer. It also explained how she could have fallen in with the Order. A pang of sympathy tightened my chest for Lola. She was a product of circumstance. She'd been led astray with the promise that the only person who really matters to her would be with her again soon.

"Well, you wouldn't have come here with him if you weren't willing to entertain her terms," I noted.

"He's curious more than anything. He doesn't think she really wants to see him," she said, rubbing her upper lip. "If you don't mind, can we get this over with? I've got other kids I need to check in on and I'm sure you've got a lot of things on your plate, too."

You have no idea. "Yes, I do. Wait here. I'll have an officer escort her brother in here and I'll get her from holding."

I passed by the conference room. Jacquie and Molly were still standing guard at the door and I caught Denise's voice carry. "What is the point of sitting here? Either they can tell us what's going on or let us go home."

"I'll be back in a few minutes. I'm just wrapping up something with our kidnapper," I said in a rushed breath to Jacquie.

I wound my way to holding. To my surprise, Lola's lawyer sat on a bench staring dazedly at his briefcase. I cleared my throat and he looked more alert. "Your client's brother is here. She's got five minutes to see him. I held up my end of the deal. She needs to help us."

He sighed again and nodded, trailing me down the row of cells to where Lola sat, picking at her nails. For her part she hadn't disappeared on me. At least she had kept her word on that. "You've got a visitor," I said, drawing her attention from her cuticles.

"You better not be lying to me, Savior," she snapped.

"I swear. Your little brother is waiting to see you."

She was on her feet in seconds, nervous energy making her bounce on the balls of her feet. She practically skipped out of the cell once the door was unlocked. The moment we were out of holding, Lola's demeanor changed. Her expression turned from excitement to solemnness and she kept her hands clasped together. At least they were still in cuffs. An icy chill of unease skittered down my spine as we entered the interview room where her brother and the social worker waited.

"Lola! I didn't think you'd really be here," the boy exclaimed, reaching for his sister the moment she appeared in his field of vision.

I had to put a hand on him to keep them apart. "I'm sorry, bud. You can talk to each other, but you can't touch," I said.

"But, why not?" Confusion turned his pubescent tenor into a whine.

"Because Lola is in some pretty serious trouble right now," his social worker said.

"Everything is going to be fine, Teddy," Lola said, locking eyes on her baby brother.

Teddy gave her a small smile and sat down across from her. I looped the handcuffs into the bar in the table.

"Five minutes," I reiterated, standing over Teddy's right shoulder.

"You didn't say anything about it being in front of you," she huffed.

"I never said anything either way." I made a show of checking my phone. "Four minutes, forty seconds."

Lola's eyes shown with tears. Her hands flexed and clenched as she fought the urge to touch her brother. "You know how much you mean to me, right?" she said, leaning as far over the table as she could.

"I know. I know you didn't mean to go away," he said.

"No, I didn't. I'm really sorry about that. But you aren't alone, Teddy. You never were. I want you to remember that okay."

A lump started to form in my stomach that had absolutely nothing to do with Taggart's magic. Her words triggered something in my head. What was it? I continued to watch the sibling exchange.

"You'll come home though, won't you?" Teddy pressed.

"I wish I could." She pulled at the cuffs on her wrists. "But I don't think I'll be able to for a while. So, I need you to be brave. You can do that, right?"

The scent of brackish water tickled my nostrils and I caught the slight shimmer of Lola's magic coalescing around her. My mouth went dry and panic set in. She was about to do magic right in front of at least two people who didn't know magic existed. There was no way I was going to let her pull a disappearing act and I started to pool my own magic around me for easy access.

Lola didn't disappear. Instead, her cheeks went pale and beads of sweat popped up along her hairline. She stiffened in her chair. I realized too late what was happening: she was using her magic to suffocate herself. My hands were numb as I fumbled for my phone to try and call an ambulance. "I need an ambulance," I said, my voice a million miles away.

I leapt over the table—my magic may have made me a little more aerodynamic than usual—and I snagged the release on the cuffs, dragging Lola's body to the floor. Her magic clogged my mouth as I opened it to try and blow breaths into her mouth while pinching her nose closed.

"What's happening?" Teddy sounded terrified. Maybe he didn't know he had magic, yet.

"Come on, don't do this to me," I said as I pressed down on her sternum.

I needed Lola to survive. I focused on that need, filling it with every ounce of power I could pool into my fingertips. I forced it into her body, past the thin layer of her own magic trying to end her life. I had no clue how I was going to explain what happened to anyone. Not to Captain Beech, not to the paramedics who were currently on route, and most of all, not to her traumatized little brother.

"What do we have?" J.T.'s voice pulled me from the life saving measures and I sunk sideways at the sight of him.

"She stopped breathing. I'm not sure if she took anything," I gave her lawyer a pointed look.

"I didn't give her anything," he said, holding his hands up as if to keep the taint of her suicide attempt away from him.

"I've been administering CPR, but so far she's not breathing," I said as J.T. moved to crouch beside me on the ground.

"You really think she took something?" He asked in a hush.

"No. She turned her own magic against herself. She used it to stop her heart or suffocate herself," I answered back. After a beat I added, "She's our kidnapper. I need her alive."

I didn't necessarily need her conscious. As going through Carly's memories had proved, I had other ways of getting information out of her. Still, letting her die wouldn't be justice for any of our missing girls.

"We'll take it from here. We're taking her to Boston Medical," he said and turned to his partner. I didn't recognize the stocky guy with a dark buzz cut.

"Get me an intubation kit," J.T. said and I stepped back to let him work.

I turned my attention to Teddy and the social worker. "Come on, you don't need to see this."

"Is she going to be okay?" Teddy whimpered.

"The paramedics are going to do everything they can," I said and led them from the room. My head swam with the realization that Lola would take her own life to protect the Order's depravity.

"Detective, there's something you need to see," someone called from down the hall.

I glanced after the officer, but didn't move. "I'm really sorry, but I need to see what's going on," I said before leaving them to accompany Lola—or not—to the hospital. As I moved back toward the bullpen, I heard a cacophony of voices. I walked faster until I found everyone crammed around one of the TVs mounted on the wall. A news anchor was talking, but the sound was off.

"What did I miss?" I asked.

"Looks like they found another one of the missing girls," the officer who'd come for me said.

TWENTY-EIGHT

Standing at the scene on the Common was Gabby—literally where they'd found Carly earlier—should have given me a jolt of relief. They'd released another girl. Whatever their motivation was for taking them in the first place, they were still being uncharacteristically merciful in letting them live.

"I saw EMTs arrive earlier. What was that about?" Molly asked as a technician looped another roll of crime scene tape to cordon off the area on screen.

"Lola tried to kill herself using magic. I don't know if she's going to make it," I answered.

"My God," she whispered. She raked her fingers through her hair. "I thought she wanted to see her brother as a condition of helping us."

"She did. I think it was to say goodbye."

"So, we're back to square one then? I mean, we

have to assume they did the same thing to Gabby that they did to Carly and you weren't able to get anything useful from her as to a location."

I watched a set of medics loading Gabby into an ambulance. She had the same wide-eyed expression Carly had worn before we went traipsing through her memory. I had no doubt if I went looking, there'd be a similar lock on her thoughts. Going for round two with whoever put the whammy on her was not high on my to do list right now. "Not necessarily," I mumbled as a thought hit me.

For all of her blustering, Lola was scared of the Order. There was no doubt in my mind that if she talked, she would have ended up dead in custody. They hadn't taken out Taggart, because he was higher up and could still be useful. Lola, though, was replaceable. Sad as it was to say, she really was. Still she'd known I was in the room. I couldn't be sure she was aware of my ability to sense magic, but she also knew it was the Solstice and my magic would be heightened.

"Uh, Ezri, are you okay? You sort of zoned out on me," Molly said.

"Yeah, I just had a thought."

"Want to share with the rest of us?"

"Well a theory anyway. I won't know until I talk to Lola."

"The same Lola who just tried to kill herself and

for all we know, succeeded? That Lola?" She said with a heavy dose of skepticism.

"I poured a lot of magic into her to keep her alive. I'm pretty sure J.T. did what he could, too," I said, starting back to the car to follow the ambulance transporting Gabby to Boston Medical.

"I know you think that made sense, but ... yeah no. You need to explain."

"I'll fill you in during the ride."

She trailed me, and by the way she slammed the passenger side door told me she was pissed. Well, she could be mad at me. If my theory was right, Lola wasn't actually working against us. At least not as much as I'd first believed. "So, what's the big thing that you zoned out for back there?"

"Okay, hear me out. Lola was working for the Order which we already knew, even if she didn't fully admit it with her lawyer present. She also knew that they have reach in the prison system. There's a reason no one has taken out Taggart. He's high up in the organization and frankly, he's a bit of a scary badass."

"How does any of this connect with her trying to kill herself?"

"She had to know the Order has eyes and ears everywhere. If she actually aided our investigation, they'd find out and if they knew it was her that led us to their doorstep, bye-bye Lola."

"She also knows you are the Savior. I'm still not

one hundred percent sure on what that means exactly, but she knew it," Molly said.

"Exactly. I'm powerful and she knows it. She also knows that the Solstice would make my magic stronger. Which means what I did to keep her alive would have a stronger chance of working. I may not have reversed the magic she used on herself, but I may have kept her alive enough and preserved her memories."

"So, you go for another memory jaunt and talk to Lola," she replied, finally following my train of thought.

"Yep."

"Works in theory, but like you said, these Order people have eyes and ears everywhere. Won't they know you've talked to her like that?"

"Not if we sneak in after visiting hours so no one spots us," I said with a devilish grin.

"I'm guessing we'll be using a little magic to keep us hidden?" She posed.

"And I think I know just the person to help with that particular part of the plan."

I SENT Molly on to find what room Gabby had been assigned while I went in search of my favorite EMT. I'd gotten a text from him letting me know he had stuck around at the hospital to talk to me. I found J.T. in the cafeteria nursing a cup of coffee. Since he just kept spinning it between his fingers, I knew he hadn't tasted a drop.

"Hey," I said, touching his shoulder to get his attention.

"Hey. I heard they found another of the missing girls," he said as I sat down beside him.

"Yeah, Gabby Freeman. She's in about the same state as Carly. I still don't get why they're letting them go. Don't get me wrong, I'm relieved to bring home living girls rather than bodies. Although from everything we know about the Order, leaving witnesses, if their minds are muddled and screwed with by magic, doesn't seem like their MO."

"Are you sure it is the Order?"

"All signs point to them being the culprits and I can't imagine they'd be pleased if their people were freelancing."

J.T. spun the cup of coffee in his fingers again and I reached over to give his hands a squeeze. He looked at me with a wan smile. "How is Jacquie holding up? Knowing they've still got her niece."

"Honestly, I don't know. I can guess that her sister-in-law is losing her shit and rightfully so. Which makes me wonder if whatever they wanted from Carly and Gabby ... maybe they found it with Neveah. If they're trying to find someone with fore-sight, I could see why they would keep looking until they got what they wanted." I had no idea if that meant she'd survive like her friends.

"We managed to get your suspect back into rhythm and breathing on a vent. Docs think she is likely to stabilize, but they aren't confident that she'll come out of the coma. I'm sorry, Ez. I know you were counting on her flipping on whoever hired her for information."

"I'm not convinced she still can't be helpful," I said, squeezing his hand again. "I am so glad you were the one who answered the call."

"I monitor the dispatch and have a friend who shunts calls involving people with magic my way. Easier that way, you know?"

"Boy do I. I need to go check on Gabby, see if I can get anything more out of her. I'm not hopeful, but you never know."

"Good luck." He kissed my knuckles before letting go.

I fired off a text to Kayla, asking her to meet me later as I headed up to find Gabby only three rooms down from Carly. I silently questioned the wisdom of keeping them so close together. Not only did that mean their families were close together—less of a concern for Gabby and Carly's parents, but still not ideal. Though it meant if someone came looking who wasn't supposed to, it'd be far too easy to find them all together.

"Everything okay with you and Mr. Paramedic?" Molly quipped.

"Yeah. He was just filling me in on Lola's condition. We'll be a go for tonight. What have we gotten from Gabby?" I answered.

"Not much. She just keeps staring at the wall, mumbling something about the darkness."

I stepped into the room to find her little brother curled up against her chest. Gabby stared blankly at the wall, just as Molly had said. Her mother sat beside the bed, her head in her hands.

"Hi, Gabby. My name is Ezri. I'm a police officer, is it okay if I ask you a few questions?" I said, pulling up a chair on the other side of the bed.

She turned to look at me and recognition washed over her. "I know you."

"That's right. From the Authority," I answered in a soft tone.

"You're friends with J.T.," she added.

"Yep. We are. How do you know J.T.?" I knew the answer already. Still if I could get her to focus on recalling information, it might help trigger something in her mind that they hadn't managed to lock away.

"He helps with healing lessons sometimes. He's nice."

"Yeah, he is. Can I ask you about what you were doing up by the mall?"

"I was with my mom and brother. We were just out walking."

"I see. And do you remember what happened next?"

She shook her head. "No. Everyone's worried about me. They keep looking at me all sad, but I don't get why."

"Because someone took you away for a little while. We were all really worried about where you were," Melissa interjected.

"I don't remember," Gabby said, rubbing her eyes.

"I know, that's okay. Why don't you try to rest? I need to talk to your mom for a few minutes," I said and gestured for Melissa to follow me into the hallway.

"Why doesn't she remember anything that happened?" She demanded once we were out of Gabby's earshot.

"Because the people that took her, the Order of Samael, locked her memory with magic. From what we've been able to determine so far, they are looking for a girl with a particular gift," I said slowly.

"What sort of gift?" She asked.

"I think it has to do with seeing the future. Does your family line have anything like that?"

"Not that I know of. Not like Claudia and the scrying," she answered, scrubbing the tiredness from her face.

"Is it possible someone thought she might have been gifted with foresight? Might she have led someone to believe it?" I knew as soon as the questions left my lips, I was going to get pushback. The way I'd phrased it made it sound like Gabby brought this on herself and that was not at all what I'd intended.

"I ... don't know. Maybe. Honestly, with two kids it's hard to keep track sometimes. Gavin has been keeping me pretty busy lately. Lying isn't something I've seen her do, but preteen girls don't tell their mothers everything. At least I didn't," she admitted.

So far it seemed like the Order had taken Gabby and Carly under the assumption they had the gift that they needed. When it turned out they were wrong, they let them go. If Adrian had somehow gotten mixed up with this, maybe he was the one tempering their usually murderous tendencies. The fact they still had Neveah worried me though. What happened if she didn't have what they're looking for? Or even worse, what happened if she did?

"Is there anything you can do about her memory?" Melissa rasped.

"I could go in and undo the magic they've done. Although I have to warn you, it won't be pretty. Everything will come back all at once. It will take time and a lot of therapy to sort through whatever she does remember."

She nodded mutely. "And what happens if you do nothing?'

"Well, she's got a memory gap of a few days.

Maybe the spell breaks down over time and she gets the memories back little by little. I won't lie, leaving it alone will be the least traumatic solution."

"But you need to know what's in her head. To find Neveah."

"We have another lead we're following," I said tentatively. I had no desire to hurt another little girl. Besides, I wasn't sure Desmond was up to the task of shepherding both girls back to mental stability.

"I know the decision is in my hands, but I want to talk to Gabby. Is that okay?"

"I can give you until the morning. If the lead we have doesn't pan out, we may need to reverse the spell anyway," I answered.

She grabbed my hands and squeezed them tight. "Thank you."

I felt awkward accepting her display of admiration. I didn't feel like I'd done much to bring her daughter home. If things went wrong with my plan for Lola, I was going to hurt her little girl more than help her.

"Get anything useful?" Molly asked as I stepped away from the room.

"Not yet. However, I have one other place to check first. Meet me at my place at ten o'clock," I said.

"You just assume I know where you live," she called after me.

"Use that big FBI brain of yours. You'll figure it out," I said and left her standing there.

TWENTY-NINE

Evening fell as I holed myself up inside my apartment, ancient ledgers stacked high on my coffee table. I'd gotten lucky months ago since the Authority had kept record of all the witches that had been hung during the trials. Maybe I'd catch a similar break and they'd have a listing of families and their magical abilities.

As I flipped through brittle pages, I sensed a presence beside me. I didn't sense Kayla's magic. Besides, the last time I'd checked my phone, she said she would meet us at 10:30. Giving me enough time to get Molly to agree fully to my idea.

"Come to tell me I'm looking in the wrong place?" I asked, setting the book down in my lap.

"Your frustration is not truly aimed at me, is it?" Theodora asked.

I brushed dark strands of red hair out of my face

and turned to look at her. "No. I just feel like I should be farther along with finding out what the Order wants and where they're keeping Neveah. Instead, I'm sitting here like a moron spinning my wheels. Trusting Lola to give up anything is a long shot. I know that, but yet I'm risking breaking into her hospital room like a criminal. All because I'm desperate and I don't want to drag the memories out of another little girl."

I slumped back against the couch and watched as the figment of my ancestor sat primly on the edge of the cushion beside me. She kneaded her hands together, her lips opening and closing as if she couldn't decide what to say.

"Sorry, I just sort of unloaded on you," I sighed.

"I think perhaps we put far too much weight upon your young shoulders," she commented.

"I used to think so, but not so much anymore. I mean, I know now that I need to rely on other people. I don't have to do it all alone."

She gestured to my clearly empty apartment. "Yet, you sit here alone."

She had a point. I could feel myself starting to creep back toward isolation. Just doing it all by myself was easier. It put fewer people in the line of fire, but I also knew neither Molly nor Jacquie would let me go running off without back up.

"It's just temporary solitude," I finally said.

Theodora pointed to the book in my lap. "I'm

afraid we did not keep as diligent records of families who did not come over with our forebearers."

"Of course not, because that would be too easy." I turned to face her. "Can I pose a question?"

"Certainly."

"From what I understand, most of us ... that is, I mean, European-descended practitioners tend to have skills related to healing and elemental manipulation."

"That would be accurate."

"I've learned that practitioners from the Afro-Hispanic community tend to be more linked to the dead."

"I thought you wished to pose a question," she arched a brow.

"Our family was different. Eleanor had the gift of prophecy, right?"

"Indeed. She had a rare gift. In fact, she once told me that only those who traveled to our land in chains bore the sight as she did. I did not understand her meaning until after her death."

"Slaves. She meant slaves." African slaves ... ancestors or at the very least distant relations of the three girls the Order had taken. I was on my feet, the ledger falling to the floor with a flutter before I realized my brain had given the signal to stand. "I have to go." The Order was looking for someone with the gift of prophecy, but you couldn't force someone to see what you wanted.

I didn't really expect Theodora to answer. After all, if her spirit or whatever manifestation had just inhabited my living room was contained in the pentacle at my neck, she didn't really have a choice and had to go along for the ride. I yanked the door open to find both Molly and Kayla standing on the other side of the threshold. Kayla eyed Molly with a wary expression. The usual purple of her pixie cut looked dull in the hallway light.

"Good, you're both here. I think I know what the Order wanted with the girls. I'll fill you in on the way."

JUNE 22, 2017

THIRTY

We made it to the hospital just after midnight thanks to Molly's insistence on driving so I could explain the plan. *Again.* I'd wanted to arrive before we lost the assistance of the Solstice—and by Kayla's glum expression she'd felt the same way—but I took the opportunity to tell them what I'd learned.

"I know what gift they thought the girls had. Foresight. Prophecy."

'But that's super rare," Kayla commented.

"I know. It doesn't even usually show up in European bloodlines. Before you ask, no I don't know how my ancestor came to have the power. It's predominately seen in bloodlines of people of color, especially those with African ancestry."

"How'd you figure all this out again?" Molly quipped as she pulled up to the back entrance to the hospital.

"It's complicated," I mumbled.

"I'm an educated woman. Give it a shot."

I tapped the pentacle resting against my collarbone. "I told you before how this was passed down through my family since the Witch Trials, right?"

"Yeah."

"Well, every woman who has worn it left behind a bit of their magic ... like a living residue. I don't know how else to explain it, but sometimes my ancestors sort of just pop up when I need them." My chest tightened at the memory of losing Eleanor Pruitt and my mother during my last big battle with the Order. "Theodora Harrow, my direct ancestor, popped in to share that bit of knowledge with me."

"They actually appear to you as full beings?" Kayla piped up from the back seat, more animated than I'd seen her in days.

"Yeah. They can do other things, like lend me their magic. Though once they do ... look all that matters is I think I know why they're after the girls. I've got a theory on why Gabby and Carly didn't make the cut. They come from mixed bloodlines. Gabby's father is Hispanic, but Carly's mom is Black. I don't know for sure, but I'd say scrying isn't the same as seeing the future."

"Which is why they tested them and let them go," Molly added. She cut the engine before looking at me. "Which means either they let Neveah go when she doesn't fit the bill and maybe we're chasing after three new girls by morning ..."

"Or she's the real deal and they are keeping her until she sees what they want her to see," I finished. I didn't want to think about what would happen if she saw something that spelled their destruction.

"Explain the part again where I fit in to all this?" Kayla prompted.

"Our kidnapper, Lola, is currently in a magically induced coma thanks to a suicide attempt. However, I think she did it so she could talk to me without the Order finding out."

"You realize that sounds crazy."

"Maybe, but it's worth a shot. Now, Agent Cartwright had a point that they might still be watching her. It's why we need to get in and out of her room unseen. Which is where you come in."

Kayla shook her head, purple strands smacking her cheeks. "No. I can't do that. I told you only really powerful Whisperers can turn the people around them invisible. Not me."

I pulled out my phone and passed it to her. Her own photo stared up from the screen. "I know Lola wasn't the only one walking through the walls of banks, Kayla."

"How'd you find out?"

"I read through Lola's file and saw your name in the system as a possible associate."

"I am in so much trouble, aren't I?"

"This was a long time ago. Some of its outside the statute of limitations. I'm willing to overlook it so long as you help me. Consider it like an unofficial confidential informant. I mean you already help out Desmond."

"Desmond saved my life by pulling me out of the shit Lola got me into. I owe him. Why do I feel like I don't have a choice with you?" She sighed. "Okay. I'll try, but this would have been easier an hour ago."

Don't I know it. At least Molly blushed in embarrassment as she realized what we were talking about. We climbed out of the car and I stared at the emergency exit in front of us. Opening the door normally would set off a ton of alarms. Still if I understood Kayla's abilities correctly, we wouldn't be touching any triggers or wires.

"Why aren't we going in the front?" Molly stage whispered as Kayla paced in front of us.

"There might be video of us entering and even law enforcement doesn't have a good reason to be here this late. We wouldn't be doing a shift change on the uniforms watching the girls or Lola this late either. Besides, I looked at the floorplan and this door puts us by a stairwell that leads up three floors to where Lola's room is and it doesn't have exterior surveillance."

"Smart."

"I didn't make Detective by accident," I muttered.

"How do we get past the guard? As you just said, she's under watch by our people."

"I can walk through walls," Kayla answered and rubbed her hands on her pants.

"Right."

"I should probably warn you this is going to feel bizarre as hell. Please remember I've never done this before. I'd say it would be easier to take you one at a time, but I can't be sure there aren't cameras inside that might pick you up. Besides, showing up randomly on security cameras without setting off alarms looks way sketchier than setting them off in the first place," Kayla said in one long breath.

"Let's get this over with," Molly said and stepped up beside Kayla.

I moved to stand on Kayla's other side and squeezed her hand, letting a little of my own magic pool between our fingers, lending her aid. I caught the ghost of a smile on her lips as fresh fruit mingled with the mundane scent of gas from the parking lot.

I wasn't sure what I was expecting when Kayla went invisible. She'd done it around me before, but I'd never really caught the scent of her magic fully, which was strange. This close, though, as she concentrated and tiny beads of sweat peppered her dark hairline, I picked up on the calming taste of lavender. In combination with my own magic, I was almost tempted to close my eyes and take a second to just rest.

The edges of the world started to blur and melt into a twisted blob of existence. I couldn't tell up from down or front from back. I could still feel Kayla's hand in mine and focused on that connection. I let her lead me in what I assumed was a forward direction. Heat and ice warred for dominance over my body as we passed through the blur of reality until suddenly, I felt something solid again beneath my feet. Blurry shapes took on meaning again as I stared up a darkened, chilly stairwell. Kayla leaned against the cinderblock wall, her cheeks flushed with exertion. Molly bent over one of the railings dry heaving.

"That wasn't so bad," I wheezed.

"You're joking right?" Molly rasped, clutching the rail for support.

"I'm with FBI lady. That sucked hard," Kayla added.

A quick glance around our confines told me there weren't any cameras in the stairwell. Which meant Kayla had time to recharge. I started up the stairs without preamble, assuming the other two would follow suit. I hit the second-floor landing before I heard the tinny echo of their footfalls on the stairs below me. We marched single file up to the third floor, pausing just out of view of the tiny square of glass at head height that gave us a glimpse at the hallway beyond.

The lighting was dimmed for nighttime rounds

and I spotted the door we needed two down from the end. An officer sat in a chair reading an actual newspaper. I almost felt bad slipping by him. After all, he had no idea that magic was about to technically make him bad at his job.

"I think we are clear to go," I hissed and gestured to the door.

Kayla peered through the tiny window, her gaze narrowing as she studied the guard. I assumed she was planning the best approach. I hoped we could avoid disturbing other patients by not traipsing through their rooms. "We will need to go past him maybe ten paces and then in," she said.

"Can I just say I'm not a fan of this," Molly said. The color still hadn't entirely returned to her cheeks.

"I'm trying," Kayla said, clearly taking her comment as a dig at her abilities.

"It's not your fault," I interjected and reached for both of their hands. The faster we got in the sooner we could get out and not have to go phasing through walls.

Kayla worried her lower lip before she gave my hand a squeeze. This time her magic seemed to tug for mine, needing it to bolster her spell. It made sense since the more time that passed from the Solstice, the less boost we had. She turned translucent and that filmy look spread down her fingers to my hand. It crept up my arm and covered the rest of me. Maybe this door wasn't as thick, because the sensation of the world turning topsy-turvy didn't hit me nearly as hard. I could almost make out the hallway on the other side of the door as we passed through it and crept past the officer on guard duty. Not even his paper rustled as our trio snuck past. We ushered single-file through the next wall. Finding ourselves in a single room with Lola laying prone in the bed, tubes and monitors hooked up and beeping steadily. She was still alive.

Molly sunk into one of the visitor chairs and hung her head between her knees. Kayla stared at the woman in the bed. I couldn't read her expression other than knowing she was conflicted. Before she could speak and draw attention from the guard posted outside, I gathered my magic before casting the same silencing spell I'd used earlier in Carly's hospital room. Satisfied that we'd have a little privacy, I approached the bed and looked at Lola's chart.

I'm by no means a medical expert, but the data seemed to indicate brain activity. So, she wasn't totally a vegetable meaning I had a shot of finding her consciousness in there and getting the information I needed.

"There was a time we used to be friends. I was the punk kid everyone teased and so we kind of gravitated toward each other. We helped each other figure out what we could do and the limits of these new abilities. She'd made what happened to me feel like fun ... until things weren't fun anymore."

"I really am sorry you had to cross paths again this way," I said, patting her shoulder.

"I hadn't heard from her in a while. Honestly, I thought she was either dead or in jail. Then you showed me that footage. I never thought she'd join up with the Order."

"She was suspected of robbing banks, Kayla. That kind of seems like the type of personality who would fit with the Order's MO," I noted.

"Not the Lola I knew."

"People change."

"Not to interrupt the therapy session, but shouldn't we get going with the telepathy or whatever you're going to do?" Molly asked, sitting up straighter.

I opened my mouth to correct her on the fact it wasn't telepathy, but realized the argument wasn't worth it. Time was precious and I was too tired to waste energy on it.

"You're coming with me, right?" I said in answer.

Molly's jaw worked in silence for a moment and I could see the uncertainty in her eyes. If I had to guess, she was warring with the more primal part of her brain. On the one hand, she needed to hear what Lola had to say to make sure I didn't misconstrue information. She couldn't have my back if she wasn't there to hear what I heard. Still, this was all so new to her and she'd already been exposed to more magic than most practitioners handle in months. She didn't have magic so even if she could accept the concept and the physical proof of it right in front of her eyes, her body wasn't hardwired to channel it the same way mine or Kayla's was. Our bloodlines gave us certain advantages normal people didn't have.

"Sure," she finally said in a pitch at least an octave higher than her usual speaking voice.

I turned to Kayla. "Do you think you can be our eyes and ears? Keep people out in case they manage to get past my silencing spell?"

Kayla nodded. "I'll do what I can."

"Thanks."

I stepped around the side of the bed and motioned for Molly to stand on the other side. She paused for a moment before doing as I'd instructed.

"Isn't it easier for me to be next to you?" She asked when I reached for her hand.

"There's a reason triangles are such a powerful shape. Three points of contact creates a stronger conduit for the magic to travel through. Take her hand."

She said nothing while taking Lola's hand with the pulse oximeter attached to her index finger. I pressed my right hand to Lola's left and swore I felt her shudder at my touch. I swallowed the lump in my throat and closed my eyes. The world felt a little less alive now that the Solstice had passed, but it still bent to my needs. Sending up a silent prayer, I focused my attention to entering Lola's mind.

At first, nothing happened. The barely lit hospital room remained around us, along with the methodical beeping of the machines prolonging Lola's life. I felt my magic rise up around me, the familiar strawberry scent calming my nerves. *I need to talk to Lola.* I knew it wasn't going to be easy—not that I'd call going into Carly's mind with Desmond's help easy—but I wasn't expecting the latent magic I'd poured into Lola's body keeping her alive to snap to attention and pull us into the woman's mind. I was grateful for the assist even if I didn't understand the mechanics of it.

The hospital room vanished, replaced by a bright white space. Lola sat in a chair in the middle, her wrists bound in handcuffs. She stared straight ahead at a point beyond the horizon. I turned to make sure Molly had made the trip. Even as a manifestation, she looked pale and worn out. She wasn't going to be able to handle much more exposure to magic without serious damage. I'd need to keep this short for all our sakes.

"Lola, can you hear me?" I called, my voice swallowed by the nothingness that surrounded us.

She didn't respond. A seed of dread implanted in my brain, worrying that she'd done too much damage to her mind and this was futile. I approached and bent down to study Lola's face. She blinked slowly as if coming out of a daze.

"Is she coherent?" Molly asked, her voice fading just like mine had. She remained at a distance.

"I don't know." I turned back to Lola and put a hand on her wrist. She tilted her head down to study the connection between our hands before she twitched, putting enough force behind the gesture to pull her hand free.

"She's got some response to stimuli, but I have no way of knowing how much damage she did to her brain," I said and stood up.

I took a step back when without warning, Lola's head snapped up and her hand grabbed my wrist. "You're running out of time to save her."

"Neveah DeWitt?" I prompted.

"You aren't looking in the right place. You're wasting your time," Lola continued.

"Tell me where to look. Help me find her. I swear, the Order won't know you helped us," I said and bent back down to her eye level. I gently placed my hand atop her left hand, hoping more of a connection would coax the information out of her.

I caught the scent of brackish water ebbing and flowing in the space around us. Instinctively, my magic rose to meet hers. She shook her head at me and I consciously tamped down on the power coursing through me. The feeling of her magic washed over me and I shivered as if I'd been hit by a wave on the beach. When her magic receded, the bright empty space around us had changed. A building rose up behind her, distorted and tilting at an impossible angle. A new smell hit me as we entered her memory—sea water. Different from the smell of her magic, but it triggered something.

Where did I smell this before?

"Carly's memory," I murmured.

"Can you give us an address?" Molly asked, finally stepping up to join me.

The memory around us wavered as Lola tried to hold tight to it, giving us as much of a glimpse as she could. I caught sight of her walking up the sidewalk, one arm draped around Gabby's shoulders. They both had a halo around them, like the kind that happens after staring at a bright light for too long. She was using her invisibility in the memory.

"We need an address," Molly pressed.

I turned to her and shook my head. "She's not going to be able to give us a street name and number. We need to look around and take note of every detail we can. This is all we're going to get from her."

Molly turned her back to me and started looking around. I'd join her in a minute, but I wasn't done with Lola. I could feel her holding on and I could also feel my own magic waning. Whatever she'd done to herself, it was making a comeback.

"I'm sorry that it had to end up like this," I whispered.

"Teddy," she croaked. Our surroundings flickered to a bedroom with a much younger version of her brother. She lay curled in bed next to him, one arm flung over his chest in a protective gesture.

"I'll look after him," I told her, hoping my words would ease her pain enough to get her mind back to Neveah's location.

"Please ... don't let them get him," she begged.

"I won't. He'll be protected. Please I need you to focus on where you took the girls. Can you do that?"

Her head slumped to the side, but the scenery changed back to the distorted building and her hazy form guiding Neveah this time. I could see the girl pulling away from Lola's grasp. *Good girl. Keep fighting.* I let go of my hold on Lola's wrists. I needed a better vantage point. At least I'd be able to do a memory recall on my own to pick up on anything I missed. I spun in a slow circle, noting the number of windows on the building—six—and the fact it didn't look to have any close neighbors. Cars lined the street with logos on high-end vehicles—an affluent area. The scene flickered on the edges, replaced by the brightness of the void we'd first entered. Lola was losing grip on her mind.

"We need to go," I said, addressing Molly.

"You're sure there's nothing else she can give us?" Molly asked.

"No. I think she held out this long just to get us this far."

I grabbed Molly's hands in both of mine and let my magic swirl up around us, taking us back to the darkened hospital room. Kayla's head snapped up when I took a sharp intake of breath as vertigo hit me. I clutched the bedrail in front of me and sucked in air until the feeling passed.

"Did you get what you needed?" Kayla whispered.

"We got something. We won't know if it's enough until we have time to piece it all together," I answered and straightened up.

I caught the spike in Lola's heart rate before it did a nosedive, sending monitors into a code situation. "We need to get out of here, now," I hissed and grabbed Kayla in one hand and Molly in the other. I dragged us toward the wall, pulling my magic down, but still keeping us secluded. Footsteps thundered down the hallway and I caught the whine of the guard vacating his seat beside the door.

Kayla's chamomile bloomed around us as she led us through the wall. We stopped short as nurses and a doctor careened into the room. We waited, none of us breathing, until I heard someone call for a crash cart. I wanted to be there when she passed, but knew it would be impossible to explain our presence without revealing ourselves. It would only lead to a world of hurt from Captain Beech and it also meant the Order might find out that Lola had survived just long enough to pass on information.

The flurry of activity in Lola's room continued and I forced myself to step forward, pulling the other two women with me back into the stairwell. Kayla's spell wrapped around us all the way down to the first floor and back out into the parking lot keeping us hidden from the prying eyes of the security cameras.

"She just died, didn't she?" Kayla rasped.

"I think so, but she didn't die in vain. She gave us something. We just have to piece it together," I repeated.

THIRTY-ONE

I stared out the passenger window at the street lights as Molly drove us back to my apartment. My brain was in overdrive, trying to compartmentalize the fact that Lola had succeeded in killing herself. Simultaneously trying to sort through what I'd seen in her memories. I also needed sleep badly.

"You can crash on my couch if you want," I told Kayla as Molly pulled up to my building.

Kayla unbuckled her seatbelt and paused, her hand on the door handle. "I think I'm just going to walk for a while. Thanks for the offer though."

She opened the door and climbed out—maybe taking us in and out of the hospital had stretched her abilities too far—then disappeared into the darkness. I exhaled and turned to Molly. "I know time isn't on our side, but I need sleep. Can we pick this up in a few hours?"

Molly's eyes were dulled by exhaustion. "Sleep is a good idea. I'll meet you at the precinct in a few hours."

I dragged myself out of the car and up to my apartment. I made it as far as the couch before I face planted and the world ceased to exist.

A MOAN ESCAPED my lips as a loud pounding filled my ears. I rubbed at my head, but the pounding continued. Struggling into a sitting position, I surveyed the apartment around me. I blindly felt for my phone which I vaguely recalled tossing on the table beside me, only 4:27 in the morning. The thudding, which my hazy brain finally realized was someone knocking on the door, continued until I staggered over and opened it.

"Do you have any idea what fucking time—" I trailed off when I saw Jacquie, hand raised and ready to smack me in the face if she hadn't been paying attention.

"Can I come in?" She asked. Her usually put-together appearance was gone, startling when my brain finally took it in and cataloged it. Her hair had been thrown into a messy bun on the top of her head and she wore sweatpants with a baggy department sweatshirt.

"Yeah, of course," I said, blinking the last vestiges of sleep from my eyes.

Jacquie being at my door this early in the morning meant one of two things, either there'd been a development in Neveah's case that somehow hadn't made it to me yet or she'd found a lead on Adrian. I prayed it was the second case. I wasn't prepared to hear bad news about Neveah.

"I'm sorry to wake you up," Jacquie said, looking anywhere around the apartment, but at me.

"It's fine. I need to head back to the precinct and meet up with Agent Cartwright anyway," I said, shoving my hands into the pockets of my pants. "What's wrong?"

"The techs did some more digging on Adrian's phone and computer. Based on the emails and texts it looks like he was communicating with someone claiming to be a distant cousin. They talked mostly about family magic related to the dead. Though, we found something you need to see."

I fought the urge to pepper her with questions as she retrieved her phone and pulled up some images. She passed it to me and I skimmed the screenshots of the email exchanges. The name on the other end of the exchange simply said Cuz. Decidedly unhelpful, especially since it didn't sound like Natalia's speech pattern. *Was there another cousin in play we didn't know about or had the Order catfished a teenage boy?*

The first few exchanges were benign enough and didn't provide anything noteworthy. Then I got down to exchanges from two weeks ago. An email from Adrian to Cuz dated June 10th: I think I found some people who can help with your problem. I can introduce you if you want. Timing might be tricky though.

Cuz responded later that same day: Do they have the backgrounds we discussed? Touch base with them about where they'll be in the next few weeks. We'll set something up.

"This sounds like he facilitated the girls' kidnapping," I said. It also sounded like someone other than a 15-year-old boy wrote the emails attributed to Adrian.

"It goes on like that. They discuss setting up a meeting to verify the information he has on the subjects of interest and they even instruct him on how to purchase a burner phone," Jacquie answered.

"I still don't understand why he'd reach out to people connected to the Order. He knows that they are bad news. I honestly can't imagine him putting these girls in danger," I added.

"He may not have known who he was corresponding with until it was too late. If he thought he was connecting with family he might have been more willing to trust them. From what we've been able to piece together based on his online activity, he was feeling pretty isolated from his father's traditions."

"It might also explain why they let Carly and Gabby go. Maybe Adrian is still involved. If he saw what they were doing to the girls, maybe he found a way to convince the Order to let them go when they couldn't give them what they wanted," I suggested.

"Maybe. We need to bring in the father again. See if he can identify who this mystery cousin might be."

"Good. I have a lead of my own to follow up on," I said, starting for the bathroom to get cleaned up.

"Why are you meeting Cartwright at the crack of dawn?" Jacquie called as I brushed my teeth and splashed water on my face.

"We paid Lola Cox a visit at the hospital," I answered, emerging from the bathroom.

"When was this?"

"About four hours ago."

Jacquie blinked. "Wasn't she in an unresponsive state when paramedics showed up at the precinct?"

"Between J.T. and my magic, we were able to stabilize her enough to keep her hanging on until I could ... mind meld with her. She gave us a distorted image of where they're holding Neveah."

"Why exactly did you decide to do this magical mind meld in the middle of the night?"

I moved to the bedroom in search of fresh clothes, stripping down as I answered. "I figured Lola attempted magical suicide as a way to pass on infor- mation without the Order being the wiser. They could have had people watching her. So, Kayla, Molly, and I slipped in under the cover of Whisperer invisibility. I figured the middle of the night was the safest time. Less foot traffic from hospital staff. Less chance of someone catching us."

"You dragged a civilian into this?" Jacquie chided.

"Hey, she's been a useful asset. Besides, she kind of owed me one. Can I catch a ride to the precinct with you?"

"There's more to this you aren't telling me," Jacquie said, but pulled out her car keys and gestured toward the door.

"You're not wrong about that," I admitted. I hadn't told her that Lola had coded and was likely now dead. Remembering my promise to keep secret that Kayla had been part of her bank robbing crew.

Jacquie waited until we were in the car and pulling onto Commonwealth Ave to speak again. "I still don't understand the logic of using a 15-year-old to lure the girls in."

"They played on his desire to know his family. I guess he managed to talk to each of the girls to see if their family had any sort of predisposition to foresight," I said.

"Honestly, I don't know if Neveah had anything like that," Jacquie said, gaze focused on the lightening sky in front of us.

"Has she ever seemed to know things before they happen?" I probed.

"Not that I can remember, but she didn't always talk to me about magic. You know how kids are. They hit puberty and think the adults in their life can't understand what they're going through." After a breath, she added, "I hate that it's true."

It also followed that if the girls had confided in anyone of their burgeoning skills, it would be someone around their own age. Someone who showed an interest in them. I just had to hope that Adrian's influence was the reason behind Gabby and Carly's release. "Would she have talked to Troy about it?"

"Maybe. They are pretty close."

"Do you think you can convince Denise to bring him by the precinct so I can talk to him again?"

"I'll try, but she's not exactly holding it together."

"I can't imagine what she's going through. To be fighting the urge to relapse due to the stress is probably just piling on more stress and anxiety."

"She won't come out and say it, but she thinks it's her fault Neveah was taken in the first place."

In a way it is. "She didn't do anything wrong."

"This time, but there's a reason Neveah didn't tell her they were sneaking out. Troy is a mess, too. He insists on sleeping in her room just in case she somehow comes back."

"We're going to get her back, Jacquie," I said.

"I want to believe you, but even if we do get her back, how much trauma will she have endured? Will we be able to give her the support she needs to heal?"

"She's your niece, Jacquie. She lived with you. She's tougher than you think."

"Thanks."

Silence fell over the car as Jacquie sped toward the precinct. I barely stifled a yawn as we pulled into the employee lot. I should have insisted we stop for coffee on the way. As if reading my mind, Jacquie reached into the backseat and pulled out a tray of large To-Go coffee cups. An audible sigh of relief escaped my lips as I took the cup she offered me and swallowed a large gulp.

"I figured if I was dragging you here before dawn, I could at least caffeinate you," Jacquie said with a small half-smile.

I chanced a look into the backseat. Her usually pristine car was filled with discarded coffee cups and a takeout container or two. She was out of the driver seat and heading inside before I turned back around. She accepted that I knew she wasn't handling this well and trusted me to say nothing. So, I didn't.

Despite the fact we still had one missing child, the bullpen was empty. I bypassed it, going straight to the conference room, downing more coffee as I went. Molly was already inside and had cleared a section of white board where she'd begun scrawling what seemed like random words like 'Prius' and 'six-story'. She'd added a few notes about time of day too.

"How long have you been here?" I asked and shut the door behind me.

Molly turned to look at me with bloodshot eyes and pale cheeks. She clearly hadn't gotten any sleep. "Since I dropped you off."

"I thought we agreed to get some sleep," I muttered.

"I tried, but I couldn't get this out of my head, Ezri. We also got the official word that Lola Cox is dead."

"Shit. Guess it was a good thing we got in when we did."

"Do you think ... what we did made her lose hold on living?"

"No, we didn't cause her to code. Her power wasn't insignificant so turning it inward did a lot of damage before either I or J.T. could do anything. We prolonged things, but we were never going to reverse it."

"You promised to look after her brother." It was a statement of fact.

"I did and I will. I'm going to make sure he understands the power he has and how to use it. I'll get him into the Authority's training programs so he can meet other kids his age."

"Are you sure that's a good idea? I mean, those classes are the very reason our girls were targeted."

My mouth went dry. I had to tell her about the additional evidence showing Adrian was involved in the abductions. "I know, but that doesn't mean the rest of the classes aren't still good. If the Order really wanted these girls, they would have found another way. However, on that note, I do have to tell you it looks like Adrian Baptiste is involved. Techs found emails on his computer talking about setting up meetings with people the other writer was interested in. It was about two weeks before the girls were taken. There was also instructions on how to obtain a burner phone and how to disappear."

She stared at me in silence. I expected her to tell me she knew he was involved or that my hope he'd been innocent was unfounded. Instead, she set the dry erase marker down, crossed the distance between us and said, "I'm sorry."

"Not your fault. Not mine either. The Order manipulated him into helping them. If there's any explanation for why they released Carly and Gabby when they didn't turn out to have what they were looking for, I have to believe it was Adrian. He may be looking to connect with a part of his heritage he's been denied, but he's not a bad kid. He wouldn't want to see the girls get hurt or worse."

"I hope you're right." She turned back to the board. "Care to add anything?"

'The smell of seawater was really strong."

"Didn't you say that Lola's magic smelled like that?"

"Sort of, but this was different. It didn't feel like magic." She arched a brow at my choice of words. "I don't have time to explain what I mean. Just believe me that it wasn't her magic."

"Could it be someone else's?"

"No. This felt like an ambient smell." It hit me as the smell tickled my sense memory. "Of course. It's got to be out near the Seaport."

"That's a big area to search."

"So let's narrow it down." I stepped up to the board and snagged the marker.

She'd already jotted down some of the details I'd picked up on. This wasn't the ideal place to go for a trip down memory lane. Even I could feel the edges of my limits starting to encroach with the more magic I used. Still though Jacquie's niece was missing and so was Adrian. Even if he was part of the problem, I owed it to his mother to bring him home if I could.

"You're about to go for a deep dive in your memory, aren't you?" Molly said from behind me.

"That I am. Sorry, but given how much magic I've been throwing around lately, it's going to be faster and easier for me to control if I go in alone."

"Not a problem. Though maybe you should sit down? In case anyone comes to check on us."

I stepped back and settled in one of the high-backed chairs. I still gripped the marker between my fingers as I closed my eyes again and willed Lola's memory to fill the space around me. The building rose up in front of me, still at a wonky angle. This time I paid no attention to the memory of Lola bringing the two girls to the place. I focused on the other sights, sounds, and smells around me. Somewhere off to my left, a seagull cawed. I heard the rumble of traffic and I caught sight of taller buildings and a glass structure that tickled my memory. Something with turnstiles stood off to the right. A sign hung up along the entrance point. I tried to move closer, but no matter how much or how fast I moved, the distance remained the same. I tried to boost my eyesight, but even that didn't help.

A firm hand on my shoulder pulled me from the memory and I looked around, ready to tell Molly I wasn't done when I saw Desmond looking down at me. He looked even more tired than I did.

"What are you doing here?" I asked, forcing myself not to shrink from his touch.

"Jacquie called me and told me you went into a suspect's mind while she was in a coma."

"I did. So what?"

"Do you have any idea how dangerous that is? If she'd slipped away while you were inside, you could have been stuck with her."

"I get that. Although, we didn't get stuck." I

didn't tell him just how close we'd come to that scenario playing out.

"She also mentioned you dragged Kayla into this?"

"It was time sensitive and we needed a way in that wouldn't attract eyes."

"You can't just make her do things she's not ready for. She's a person Ezri, not a tool to be used."

I turned to Molly. "Can you give us a minute?"

She left the room, the door shutting behind her. I spun in the chair to face Desmond. "You know Kayla has a criminal history, right?"

"Yes, of course I do. We met while I was on the job. You know that."

"So, you're mad I treated her like a confidential informant?"

"But she isn't one, Ezri."

"I needed to know what Lola wasn't telling me when the Order could be listening in. So, I did what I had to do. I still have a little girl who is out there. She's scared. They're doing who knows what to her to try and get her to see some vision of the future they want her to see. So yeah, I may push people a little out of their comfort zones, but I'm not stopping until I bring her home."

Desmond opened his mouth to say something, but shut it again and shook his head. He rubbed at his stubble and turned his back to me. When all of this was over, I needed to check in with him about what was going on in his head. *Could he be suffering magical burnout, too? Is he pushing himself too far by helping me?*

"Do you think you're any closer to finding her?" His voice pulled me out of my mental spiral.

"I think so. The building Lola showed us, the one where they are keeping Neveah, is somewhere near the Seaport. There's a big building with turnstiles but I can't see the name on the building."

"The Aquarium," he offered.

That's it! "How did I not recognize it?"

"There's hundreds of buildings around there, Ezri. With quite a few hotels they could be in."

"Not a hotel. The room where they'd kept Carly was soundproof. Hell, there wasn't even a vent to get air in. Definitely not something that comes standard in a luxury hotel. Plus, the building only had six floors. Which actually gives us a way to find them!"

"I still don't like how you got the information," he muttered.

"Des, you don't have to like it. Still I did what I had to do to get a real, viable lead to find these kids."

He rubbed at his face. "You're not the one who has to try to rebuild their minds."

"I know," I answered softly. "I'm sorry this is taking such a toll on you. I want to help. Just tell me how."

"There's not much you can do. You may be the Savior, but even you have limits and so do I. I guess

I'm just realizing they're a lot closer than I'm comfortable with. I don't know that I'll actually be able to help them in the way they need."

I grasped my cousin's arm. "You're exactly who they need. I think Gabby may be easier. I didn't touch her mind so it's all locked away. Maybe she won't remember."

He gave me a tired, sad smile. "Maybe that's better or maybe it will create trauma all its own when she realizes her best friends underwent something that she can't remember. I want to try group therapy with them to see if their shared experience can provide a way for them to heal.'

"We need to find Neveah first," I sighed.

"I can help you look," he said and pulled one of the chairs away from the table.

"No. Molly and I need to do this. They took the girls, because they thought they had the gift of foresight. They found them, because of Adrian."

"What?" He slid into the chair anyway.

"We have evidence to prove he was involved. He may not have known exactly what he was doing. Still he told the Order about these girls and helped figure out where they'd be so Lola could grab them. They gave him instructions on how to disappear."

"Shit," he swore.

"I know. Jacquie is bringing in his parents now to see what else they can tell us. This is going to break Belladonna's heart."

The conference room door swung open and Molly stuck her head back in. "Sorry to break this up, but I think I have an idea of how we might find them."

I was on my feet and halfway to the door before saying, "We need to look near the Aquarium."

Desmond stayed seated. He clearly needed some time to hash out his own feelings on everything. I followed Molly to one of the computers at an unused desk in the bullpen. She'd pulled up a street view map of the city. Her fingers flew over the keys and the Aquarium pixelated into view. She started manipulating the settings until we were facing the Aquarium in the same direction I'd seen it in Lola's memory.

"Can we back up a little? It was farther away than this ... like, I could kind of see it off to the left," I said.

Molly fiddled with the settings again as raised voices filtered through the empty bullpen. I craned my neck to see Jacquie trying to corral Mr. Baptiste into an interview room. He was shouting in a language that sounded vaguely French—Creole maybe—and gesturing to Belladonna who followed after them in silence. Even from this distance I could see her jaw set in determination.

"That's going to be ugly," I murmured.

"It's never easy to find out someone you love has

done something heinous," Molly answered and leaned back. "That better?"

I studied the screen. "Yeah. Start turning to the right."

The mouse's scroll button whirred and the image shifted. I tilted my neck to the right, trying to get the perspective from Lola's memory. "Stop!" I pointed to a building whose façade looked like the one we'd seen.

"It looks like it's a luxury apartment complex owned by a bunch of different companies," Molly said as she input the address into the system.

"Probably all of them really owned by the Order."

She reached for the phone. "I'll get a team together."

I put my hand on the receiver to stop the call. "We can't take a team in there."

"We can't just go in alone," she quipped. "We need back up."

"They are going to be throwing around who knows how much and what kinds of magic. You really want to expose your people to that, because I sure as hell don't want to do that to my fellow officers."

"We can't mount a rescue with two people, that's insane."

I glanced in the direction Jacquie had gone. "We won't. If you can convince your team to stay outside, let us go in for the breach then that's fine. Although they have to stay out of the line of fire."

"Okay. I got it. However, that still leaves just the two of us going in against an unknown number of assailants."

"Trust me, it won't just be the two of us," I said and fingered the pentacle at my throat.

I wasn't sure how it worked exactly, other than their magic coming to life could sacrifice itself to help me. Somehow, I knew that any of the women whose power lived in the metal would do that for me. Though I also knew that once it was gone, I couldn't harness it anymore. I needed to preserve as much as possible, but I had a hunch Theodora would be willing to give herself up to save a child.

I reached the interview room and knocked sharply two times. I heard the scrape of metal against the cement floor and Jacquie appeared in the doorway.

"I need you," I said softly.

"I'm just starting to get them to open up about who Adrian could have contacted."

"We found where they're keeping Neveah. We need to move now and I'm not doing this without my partner."

Jacquie glanced back at the people sitting in the room. "Okay. Give me two minutes."

Nervous energy coursed through me and an electric current jumped along the tiny hairs on the back of my arms as I headed to get suited up. I'd felt like this the last time I'd faced down the Order. I'd had more magical firepower on my side at the time. I wouldn't risk Desmond or Kayla like that again. I had to trust that Molly and Jacquie had my back and the magical boost of my ancestors' magic would be enough.

Morning sun slanted through the windows of the six-story building. We'd parked half a block away and insisted the FBI agents ride with our patrol in unmarked cars. We couldn't be sure what floor the Order occupied—although if it were me, I'd be as high up as possible for the best vantage point—and that meant we couldn't risk them catching a glimpse of black SUVs and flashing lights.

"How exactly are you intending to keep all of these officers out of the line of fire?" Jacquie asked, now wearing jeans and a t-shirt under her tactical vest.

"I'm still working on it." I stepped closer and put a hand on her shoulder. "You don't have to come in with us."

She fixed me with her trademark glare. "Ezri, I know what might be waiting in there. It terrifies me, but I know a familiar face will make things easier." She lowered her voice even though the closest person was at least two feet away. "As much as you might like Agent Cartwright and so far she hasn't lost her mind with all the magic stuff ... I don't trust her to have your back in this."

I didn't say it out loud, but I appreciated her backing me up on this all the same. I turned my attention to the building in front of me. On the outside it looked unassuming. Just another block of businesses nestled in the Seaport, but I could feel the darkness emanating from within. With that much concentrated power there was bound to be heavy hitters. I wondered if they knew Lola was dead or if they even cared. She, like so many, was expendable to them.

"What's the call, Detective Trenton?" Molly asked, leading her team of agents to where Jacquie and I stood.

Showtime. "We're going to proceed in teams of three. We three will take top floor and the rest of the teams will work their way down. If you find our targets, do not engage. Radio for back up immediately. They are to be treated as armed and extremely dangerous."

I got nods of understanding all around. Officers and agents began breaking into trios, leaving Jacquie, Molly and I to make the initial breach. Making sure there were no prying eyes, I pressed my fingers to the pentacle on the chain around my neck and felt it warm with the promise of magic. I took a centering hit from the sandalwood charm beneath it. No sense going in with my senses all muddied.

"How confident are you that they are on the top floor? We didn't get any indication of that from Lola's memories," Molly questioned.

"It's tactically smart and I think I may have seen something in Carly's memory about being up high. These guys are assholes who think they are above everyone else. They would want to be as high as possible to see their enemies coming."

"Then maybe we could have used that invisibility thing now," she muttered.

I stopped myself before I reminded her—in less than nice terms—how dangerous that would be for Kayla. Desmond was already pissed at me for using her to get into the hospital. If I'd tried to use her to get an entire police force into a building unseen, he'd murder me. Instead I said, "We just have to be on guard."

Taking a deep breath, I signaled for the other teams to breach from the back of the structure. If we came at them from both sides it might throw them off enough to give us the upper hand. Moving with as much confidence as I could muster, I led my team through the front door and the adjacent stairwell. I couldn't make us invisible. Still I could muffle our approach so as soon as the door swung shut behind

Molly, I cast a spell to quiet our footfalls on the metal risers. Gun pointed ahead, I rounded the first landing. I don't know what I was expecting, but no one waited for us as we made our ascent. The absence of an offense should have made the tiny hairs on the back of my neck stand at attention, but I was too focused on getting in.

"Look out!" Jacquie grabbed the collar of my shirt and yanked me back to the relative safety of the fifth floor landing. A fireball slammed into the stair above where I'd been standing, marring the metal and increasing the temperature in the confined space by a good twenty degrees.

"Looks like our fire throwing friend is back," I hissed to Molly.

"You think he might have a change of heart if we tell him his friend is dead?" She replied.

"Something tells me he's not gonna care," I said coughing as smoke billowed above us. *That's strange, there shouldn't be anything to burn in here.* Sucking in a breath, I darted off the landing and up a few steps to where I'd been before. The scorch marks warmed the soles of my shoes as I inched my way toward the next landing.

Golf-ball sized fireballs peppered the air around me and I pressed myself to the wall. Sweat prickled along my hairline and it wasn't just from the heat. I should have anticipated something like this. A few more well-placed fireballs would require fire response and the other teams on the lower floors would be in even greater danger.

"You have a plan to get past this guy, Ezri?" Jacquie called from below.

Not one that doesn't end in more dead bodies. "I'm working on it," I muttered as the radio on my belt crackled to life.

"First floor clear," the team leader reported in.

I reached down with one hand, weapon still trained on the stairs above me and said, "Acknowledged."

Smoke began to obscure my vision, forcing me to take a step back and think. This shouldn't be a hard problem to solve. So why was I so apprehensive about moving forward?

"Calm yourself," Theodora's voice said in my ear or maybe it was in my head, because when I turned she wasn't there. Even still, I did as she ordered and centered myself.

I could do this. I was the damn Savior after all. I'd accepted that mantle with all of the additional responsibilities and skills that it entailed. I had the power to protect my friends. I needed to use it. The Order knew we were already here. Maybe my silencing spell hadn't been strong enough or maybe they had security cameras. Either way, we'd lost the element of surprise and keeping that spell going was pointless. So, I held my free hand out in front of me, redirecting the energy to create a translucent barrier that reached from wall to wall. I advanced around the corner and a fireball smashed against the barrier, but it didn't break through.

"Come on," I stage whispered to the rest of my team.

Jacquie and Molly appeared, guns raised. I pushed onward, fireballs sizzling against my magic. Every hit kicked off sparks that smelled like flambéed fruit. Through the haze of smoke, I caught a figure retreating through a doorway and I pressed on. Assuming our fiery friend had grabbed the door handle while still burning hot, I kicked the door open. It slammed against the wall with a concussive 'bang,' but the hallway was clear of smoke and I sucked in a greedy breath as soon as my feet touched carpet.

"Second floor clear," a female voice echoed over the radio on my hip.

I reached for it to turn it off, but stopped. It was better we knew for certain we were on the right floor. After all, the Order could have lured us to the top floor assuming we'd split our forces. Obviously mundane cops and agents would be no match for the literal firepower being lobbed around up here.

I gestured for Jacquie and Molly to start checking rooms while I advanced down the hallway, making sure to keep the shield ahead of us. We moved methodically, doors banging open as they cleared the rooms along the way. Our fire starter had vanished. I centered myself with the sandalwood charm, clearing my senses from the clash of magic until I could follow the ashy scent of his magic. Not unlike the scent of a Fire Haunt's magic, but those beings were the spirits of long-dead dark practitioners killed during the Witch Trials. Our guy was very much alive. The trail weaved around a corner toward the back of the building and I pressed myself to the wall, inching around slowly with my weapon trained in front of me.

A bright blue ball of flame the size of a basketball zoomed toward the barrier, smacking into it with a force that made me stumble. He was upping his game which meant we were getting closer. I peered around the corner again and watched him flex his fingers. Letting an extra bit of will out into the spell, I created a tiny hole right in front of me, just big enough for a bullet to travel through. My target seemed preoccupied as I aimed and squeezed off one shot.

The yelp of pain and sudden lack of fireballs told me I'd hit my target. The hole in my shield reformed, and I watched as he cradled his bleeding hand to his chest. I could smell burning flesh as he pressed one hand to his palm. *Is he trying to cauterize the wound? Gross.* He'd survived the wound, but it took him out of commission long enough for us to advance. Stepping out of the protective bubble of the shield was risky. Although with our main adversary out of the way, I was willing to take the chance. Between one heartbeat and the next, the spell dropped away. Tiny black dots populated my vision and I staggered sideways as exhaustion hit me hard. Trying to shake it off, I blinked until my vision cleared.

Jacquie was already ahead of me, cuffing the guy to a nearby door handle. She may have slammed his head against the door to render him unconscious, but I wasn't going to say anything. Her anger and need to mete out punishment on anyone connected with her niece's disappearance was a feeling I knew all too well. She'd have let me get it out of my system. The least I could do was return the favor.

"This going to be a problem, Agent Cartwright?" Jacquie eyed Molly, weapon at her side.

"He attempted to assault multiple law enforcement officers. You subdued him in the course of entry," Molly answered.

We'd been standing in front of a set of robust metal double doors for nearly a minute and no one else had come out to greet us. The Order had more than enough lackeys to throw at us, but the teams on floors three through five hadn't reported in yet. As if on cue, garbled crackling emanated from the radio at my belt.

"Floor four, we're taking fire," a strained male voice called.

"It's your call, do we breach here or do we go

down and check it out?" Molly said, gesturing to the door in front of us.

I looked from the door to the hall and the way we'd come. I thought I'd been ready for this responsibility, but I wasn't prepared to risk the lives of my brothers and sisters in blue. Not to magic they didn't understand. There was still a chance that whatever was going on two floors below us was the true diversion.

"We stay here," I said and landed a kick to the door. It buckled easier than I expected. A second kick bent the lock enough to allow us entry.

I pushed through first, gun raised. I inhaled and didn't pick up any traces of unfamiliar magic or any magic for that matter. Still that didn't mean they hadn't been here. For all we knew, they'd managed to go down a back staircase without using magic.

"I need you two to buy me a minute or two. I need to try something," I said.

The echo of shots ricocheting over the radio frequency prompted me to remove the device from my belt and hand it to Jacquie. "Whatever you're going to do, you need to act fast," she said.

Much like I'd done at Park Street three days ago, I let the world's magic snap to life around me. It showed me the after images of what had come before us. I saw our Firestarter friend racing out of the room, tiny tendrils of magic sparking from his fingertips. I heard the ghost of voices coming off to the right. I followed it and found a spacious bedroom devoid of any furniture. The door to what I assumed was a walk-in closet sat ajar. Thick carpeting muffled my approach and I nudged the door open to find nothing, but empty hangers lining both sides of the closet.

"They're fucking with us," I said and returned to the main room. "I don't think they were ever up here."

Jacquie opened her mouth to speak, but she never got the words out. The ground beneath us shook and a deafening explosion erupted. Glass shattered around us. The blast knocked me sideways and I slammed into a wall. My shoulder ached instantly and spots danced in my vision. At least I knew it wasn't magic burn out this time. The air grew thick with smoke, dust, and debris. I struggled to my feet, my left arm hanging useless at my side. I didn't bother looking to see how extensive the damage was. It didn't matter. I needed to find my allies and fast.

THIRTY-THREE

My hearing returned in bits and pieces, high tones hitting my brain first followed by the lower register. Through the fog I spotted Jacquie gripping her right leg. I staggered to her side.

"Can you move?" I'm sure my voice was far louder than necessary, but if my hearing was this affected, hers probably was too.

She looked up at me. "It might be broken," she shouted.

I pressed my good hand to her leg and she let out a strangled cry audible even to my damaged eardrums. "Hold still."

My magic bloomed around me, a welcome scent in the ashy confines around us. I wasn't a healer, but I could still help. I willed the bone and muscle to knit itself back together. She'd still need to get it looked at and properly splinted, but I didn't have time for that.

"Agent Cartwright," Jacquie coughed, sound returning to normal.

"Molly!" I shouted.

"Here," she answered weakly.

I followed the sound of her voice and found her near one of the exterior windows. She had a large gash on her forehead, cascading blood down her nose. I couldn't assess if it was just superficial or if there was more extensive damage.

"Can you stand?" I asked, offering her my good arm.

She took it and to my surprise was able to pull herself up without too much issue. She swayed against me and the wound in her head gushed heavily. I extended the healing magic to her head and she blinked.

"Thanks."

Behind us Jacquie limped toward the doorway. "We haven't had contact with the other teams. We need to check in."

I reached for my radio when I remembered I'd taken it off to avoid the distraction of the gunshots. *What happened? Did they set off an explosive?* "This is Detective Trenton to all teams. Report in," I said once Jacquie returned my radio.

"Team five, we're trapped on the fifth floor. Stairs are out, but we're all okay," the leader answered.

"Team two, we're out. EMS is on route," another officer replied.

My breathing started to normalize again. "Copy."

"Team one. We're clear, too."

Leaving teams three and four unaccounted for. My chest constricted as they failed to report their status. After an interminable silence, the leader of team three said, "We've got one injured."

"Team four, come in," I ordered, gripping the device tight enough to turn my knuckles white.

No answer. We needed to move. Now. "Come on, we're going down there."

"How do you expect us to do that? We have no idea if the floor beyond this room is even stable. The safer option is to report our location and let EMS come to us," Molly said.

"No. They've got Neveah. She could be hurt down there," Jacquie argued.

"You're not going to do her any favors if you get injured more than you already are trying to rescue her," Molly argued.

"I'm with Jacquie. We move. You can stay if you want, but I'm not waiting around. They purposely did this to hide something. I'm not letting them get away with it."

I pushed the metal doors outward and winced as pain lanced through my injured shoulder. Gritting my teeth, I turned the spell I'd used on Molly and

Jacquie inward. Heat radiated from my shoulder blade down to the tips of my fingers. I doubted if I could bear any weight on the arm, but it didn't make me want to scream in agony with every step. It would have to do.

Our handcuffed Order lackey lay sprawled on the ground, still unconscious. I knelt to check for a pulse and found it throbbing strong and steady in his neck. "Teams one and two, be advised we have a detained hostile on floor six near the back stairwell. Be sure to send EMS up here."

I didn't wait for a response. I knew I should have let them know we were on the move, but I didn't care. We'd rendezvous with Team Five soon enough. We retraced our steps back to the stairwell we'd used. I peered down to the next floor. It appeared clear, but I noticed smoke billowing from the landing below it. Jacquie grasped the rail along the wall with both hands as she hobbled down the stairs as fast as her still-injured leg would allow.

"I'll get her, Jacquie. I promise," I said, hoping she understood that she didn't need to come with us if it was too painful.

"I'm fine, Trenton. Now, move your ass."

We made it to the fifth floor. While being an undignified trio covered in grime, blood, and injuries, we cleared the floor as we went. Finally finding our team members huddled by the opposite stairwell.

"Do we know what happened?" I asked as we joined the huddle.

"No idea, Detective," one of the uniformed officers answered. She had a cut over her left eyebrow, but for the most part she looked unharmed.

"We got the report that Team Four was taking fire and we went to assist. Before we could make it down, the whole building shook," one of the jacketed FBI agents on the team added.

"Why go to all this trouble over a missing kid?" The third member of the team asked before noticing Jacquie among us. "I didn't mean any disrespect, Detective. I know the missing kid is your family. I just meant ..."

"I know what you meant. Blowing up a building to hide an abduction is fishy and doesn't fit the M.O. they'd previously established with the other victims," Jacquie answered flatly.

I pushed through the group and studied the door to the stairs. It appeared sealed shut, but a blast from below wouldn't have done that. I concentrated and picked up the scent of onions all over the door. Someone had magically sealed it. They'd known we would be searching each floor and they wanted to make sure we were kept from help for as long as possible.

"Nice try," I muttered and let my own magic find the edges of the spell in front of me. It wasn't difficult to find—probably because it was shoddy work—and in less than a minute, I'd dismantled it. The door swung open like it was newly installed.

"Detective, we should wait for EMS," the FBI agent called after me.

"Trust me, Forrest, you aren't going to convince her to stay put," Molly addressed the agent and then followed right after me.

Jacquie brought up the rear. I didn't hear any other footsteps so I assumed the other officers were waiting for EMS. Ultimately, it was probably safer for everyone involved. Heat rippled in the air as we approached the fourth floor. I held my good arm up to shield my face and stumbled back as a ball of flame—larger and more dispersed than anything our friend from floor six had managed—erupted just beyond the door onto the floor.

"You really sure you want to go in there?" Molly coughed.

I don't have a choice. "I'll be fine." Yanking the door open, I ducked as low as I could and rushed into a burning inferno.

THIRTY-FOUR

I'd never felt anything quite like the blaze around me. For a brief moment, I wondered if this was what Hell felt like? Shadows shimmered in the heat around me, playing tricks on my eyes until I couldn't tell whether there were actually people near me.

In the distance I heard the wail of sirens, no doubt the fire department come to extricate us. We may have lost three good officers and agents today—no normal person could withstand this heat, especially if they'd been near the center of the blast—but I'd be damned if I lost a child.

"Neveah! Call out!" I yelled as loud as I could above the roar of the flames.

I got no reply. I refused to believe that meant I was going to find four bodies. I ended up on my belly, crawling awkwardly on my good arm to conserve oxygen and avoid the blistering heat higher in the hallway. I didn't know how I knew where to go, but advanced to the far end of the hall to the room that sat two stories below the apartment we'd been in. The blast had warped the doors here and they sat askew on badly melted hinges. Simmering onions now filled my nose as I slithered into the room. The spell caster was either nearby or had used magic very recently in the room.

The smoke was thinner here. Now I knew what the spell had done. They couldn't completely hide themselves from the after effects of the blast, but they could minimize it. I followed the trail of magic into the bedroom. My foot had just crossed the threshold when I spotted movement out of the corner of my eye. I barely dodged the incoming fist.

It belonged to someone I didn't recognize, a stocky man with thinning sandy hair and watery brown eyes. His shirt was torn and the Order's brand shone red against the skin of his bicep.

"I don't have time for this bullshit," I snapped and used the butt of my gun to cold cock him upside the head. It wasn't elegant and probably wasn't the approach he had assumed I'd take, but it worked. He crumpled to the ground and didn't move.

A fresh sheen of sweat prickled along the hem of my shirt and under my arms as I approached the walk-in closet. This one didn't have hangers like the one two floors above. Instead, at the midway point was a very large door with a keypad lock. Part of me wanted to smash it, but I knew that could mean whatever—or whoever—remained inside would be stuck. So, I studied the keypad, wishing in that moment for something to give me a hint for tight combination.

"Focus," I told myself, blocking everything else out.

The sounds and smells of the blaze in the hallway vanished as did the uneasy cracking sounds of the structure around me threatening to give way from the damage. The keypad glowed bright in my vision and I pressed my palm to it. Like a palm reader, tendrils of green vines slithered out of my fingertips into the machine. All of a sudden it clicked, releasing the door.

It took several tries to heft the damn thing open, but when I did, I found Neveah on a cot tightly curled around a flimsy pillow. I bent down beside her and pressed the hand from my good arm to her throat looking for a pulse. She startled upright, eyes wide and mouth hanging open in a silent scream.

"Neveah," I said, hoping she wasn't too traumatized to recognize her own name.

She blinked up at me. "I know you. You're Aunt Jacquie's partner ... the Savior."

I gave her a smile. "That's right. We've come to take you home."

Leading her out of that tiny cell back into the inferno wasn't my brightest move. But she held tight to my hand, lending me a little of her own magic to help get us through. It felt like she knew I needed it before I did. A comfortable bubble of fresh, cool air wrapped around us, letting us move unobstructed through the mess to the stairwell where Jacquie and Molly waited.

The moment we stepped into the stairwell, Neveah let go of my hand and flung herself at her aunt. They held on to each other for a solid minute before we traipsed back up a floor and reunited with Team Five just in time for fire rescue to come barreling down the opposite end of the floor. One turnout-gear clad firefighter led us back the way they'd come and out into the late morning air. I'd never thought Boston air tasted so good.

"You need to have the paramedics check you out," the firefighter ordered our group and pointed to a cadre of ambulances blocking the road.

I scanned the faces of the waiting EMTs, but J.T. wasn't among them. I couldn't expect him to be everywhere when I needed medical attention. He was my boyfriend not my personal healer. Not that having a personal healer wouldn't have been awesome. So, I had to settle for getting my arm poked and prodded by a regular medic and shipped off to Boston Medical with everyone else. I overheard one of the medics commenting that Jacquie was lucky her leg injury wasn't worse. Maybe my healing skills weren't as bad as I thought.

MORNING TURNED to afternoon as I sat in a hospital room with my arm in a sling. I'd gotten off lucky and we all knew it. Even if I couldn't explain how I'd miraculously not suffered graver injuries, especially racing into fire without any protective gear. I'd ditched the oxygen mask as soon as the nurses left me alone. Jacquie hobbled in on crutches with Molly behind her with a large bandage on her forehead.

"What you did was insanely reckless and stupid," Molly accused.

"As I recall, you didn't stop me. You even told one of your people it was pointless to try," I answered.

"How exactly are we supposed to report all of this? Do we even know if what caused the explosion was mundane or magical?" Her voice dropped to a barely audible whisper on the last word.

"We have other people in the know on the force and in other departments. If it's magic-based, we'll know about it. In the meantime, do we have any word on Team Four?"

The fact that neither Jacquie nor Molly met my gaze told me everything. "Damn it."

"They found another body on the floor, too. Burned pretty bad, but it looked like it might be an African American teenager. They did a rush DNA test and it looks like it's a match for Adrian Baptiste," Molly said.

My heart sank as her words hit me. I'd started this whole damn week off reassuring Belladonna that I'd bring her son home to her. Now all I could give her was the heartbreaking news that she'd lost her only child. I couldn't even bring myself to tell her why. Knowing he had some involvement—however unwitting—in the Order's plot to kidnap Carly and the other girls would break her.

"I'll make the notification to the family once they release me," I said somberly.

"You don't have to do it alone. I'm lead on the case, remember?" Jacquie added.

After a beat, I said, "How's Neveah?"

"Resilient considering everything she's been through. It doesn't seem like they wiped her memory at least not like they had with the other girls. Either they didn't have time or ... they weren't done with her yet."

"Do you think she's up for some questions?"

"Well that's up to Denise, but if I know my sister-in-law, she'll want to let Neveah rest."

Leaving me with mustering up the courage to face Mr. Baptiste and Belladonna. Part of me hoped the doctors would keep me indefinitely so I wouldn't have to face that horror show. Too soon a blue scrub-clad doctor came by discharging me and Jacquie. Neither of us was in good enough shape to drive on our own so Molly brought us back to the precinct. Apparently, Adrian's parents had been waiting there all morning. I slid into a chair and took a deep breath.

"We have some news. We found Neveah DeWitt. She's back with her family, but we found evidence that Adrian was involved in the abduction." I held up a hand to keep both of his parents quiet. "We don't think he knew what he was doing, but the Order of Samael used him to lure the girls. Unfortunately, we found a body in the aftermath of Neveah's rescue."

Belladonna let out a wail and clutched at her ex-husband's arm. I expected him to push her away, but instead he held her tightly. "You think it is our boy?" His voice came out in a whisper.

"Preliminary DNA results say yes. I'm so very sorry for your loss."

"Can we see him?" Belladonna's tone was stronger than her ex-husband.

"The body was very badly burned. I don't think that's a good idea," Jacquie added.

"I'm so sorry I wasn't able to bring him home to you," I whispered, not meeting Belladonna's eyes.

"You told me you couldn't make promises. Now I know why. I don't blame you, Ezri. I blame myself. He pulled away from me and I let it happen. Now ... he is gone."

I wanted to tell her not to blame herself, but I

couldn't when I was doing the same thing. If I'd pushed Lola harder or sooner, maybe I could have saved him, too. I just had to hope that Neveah could give us enough to punish someone for all of the losses.

LEAVING Adrian's parents to grieve, we returned to the hospital and stopped outside Neveah's room. Two uniformed officers greeted us with silent, solemn nods. Neveah sat up in bed the moment I walked through the door. Her eyes were bright, not haunted like her friends. She retained the memory of everything the Order had done to her and yet she could still find it in her to show positive emotions.

"Hi, Neveah. How are you feeling?" I sat at the foot of her bed.

Having a nasal cannula in for oxygen made her voice sound strange. "Are Carly and Gabby okay?"

"Yes. They're here, but they don't remember what happened to them. Do you?"

She nodded. "Yes. They tested us. They wanted to know if we had a gift in our blood."

"To see the future?" I prompted.

Another nod. "Carly and Gabby didn't have it."

"Did you know that before they took you?"

She lowered her gaze. "Maybe. Though we

thought we could find a way for all of us to get it. Like how we wanted to all be healers."

"I see."

Denise put a hand on her daughter's arm. "Can't you ask your questions later? She's just been through hell. She needs to rest and recover."

"Understanding what she remembers and knows about who took her will help us stop them," I answered.

"It's okay, Mom. I need to tell her what I saw."

"You had a vision?" I leaned forward, not wanting to miss anything.

"Sort of. I saw something, but I heard something too. It sounded like me, but not me. I don't know how to explain it."

"What did you hear and see, Neveah? It's really important that you remember as much as you can."

"It was winter time and you were facing a monster. It was like Death, but not." She rubbed at her eyes. "The voice said 'When Darkness reaches its height, and Death's child reigns, the last of Harrow's blood must flow forever more or the life blood of the world will be no more.' Do you know what that means?"

I couldn't even begin to decipher Neveah's words. All I knew is it meant I'd be doing some more heroics before the year was through. I just had to hope I had enough time to prepare and figure out what price the world now asked of me.

QUICK AUTHOR'S NOTE

GETTING this book out in the time I did was actually quite the feat. I'd set myself the goal of finishing it by October 2019 and I managed it, even with a tiny baby to take care of. Having a child has changed my life in so many ways but I'm so grateful to have him. Even if he tries to steal the computer when I'm writing. After the length of time it took me to write, rewrite (again and again) and publish book 1 in this series, I'm thrilled that this book came together so quickly. I owe a lot of that to Rebeca Heyman, the developmental editor who changed the way I approach writing series.

Coming into the second book in the series, I wanted to expand the universe and dive a little into some of the side characters. Which is why we got to meet Jacquie's family. There's still a lot we don't know about Detective DeWitt, but I promise it's coming....

I wanted to give a special thanks to my beta readers: Angela, Kathryn and Molly for giving me really helpful feedback to make the story even better. And to Kathryn, Jason and Mark for giving life to some of the characters that populated this story.

I would be remiss if I didn't offer up a kudos to the lovely Alecia, my editor. Not only does she do fantastic work but she's easy to work with and gives suggestions that make the narrative stronger. I look forward to her helping shape the rest of this series for everyone!

You might have noticed that Summer's Stolen ends on much more of a cliffhanger than book 1, and yes, I did that on purpose! You didn't think Ezri was done facing down magical obstacles did you? Book 3, Autumn's Legacy, is a fun romp and if you want to catch a glimpse of what magic awaits her, turn the page to find out more...

Sarah Biglow is a *USA Today* bestselling author. She lives in Massachusetts with her husband and son. She is a licensed attorney and spends her days combatting employment discrimination as an Investigator with the Massachusetts Commission Against Discrimination.

You can find an up-to-date list of all my books here

www.ingramcontent.com/pod-product-compliance
Lightning Source LLC
Chambersburg PA
CBHW060655190726
48289CB00002B/426